Sound
of the String

An African Bush Country Adventure

BRAD ISHAM

ISBN-10: 0615557457
EAN-13: 9780615557458

Dedication

To Amber, thank you for knowing I could before I did and not
letting me fail to start. Thank you for sharing my life and for being
with me to discover Africa. I love you. Of course, much of this book is you.

To my older brother, a decorated veteran, taught to kill at too young an
age. He did it well. It did him in. At times his tongue was sharp and
cutting, and the pain of his words lasted like scars remembered long after
the offense. At times he was soft and kind and poetic and
you could see the parts of his soul that were broken. By the end of our time
he left me with something of great value, lessons. He had undefeatable
demons. I hope God understands. Another 1st Cavalry
Crazy Horse gone to pasture.

Acknowledgements

Dennis Kamstra was the first person in the hunting industry to tell me my writing was good. Thanks for the encouragement, the hunts we shared, breaking my video camera to prove your new monopod was a great buy, and your friendship.

Rean Steenkamp was the first to publish me in his *Africa's Bowhunter* magazine. Thanks for the space over the years, your time, and your friendship.

Gerri MacDonald, Pieter and Pikkie Van Aardt, and Daniel the tracker, all of you make Africa what it is to me.

Dail Willis made editing a pleasure and made sense of my rambling, run-on sentences and overuse of the word and. You're a peach, Dail.

Foreword

The Sound of the String

When a mindful hunter looses an arrow from a well-crafted longbow, the string is the only sound he hears. As it launches the arrow forward, powered only by the straightening of bent limbs, the string parts the air to impose its will upon the shaft.

When the string is the only sound it means everything is true between the bow and the bowman.

Hearing the quick whisper of the string in the quiet of the bush can be a beautiful ending to a life well lived or a betrayal of a hunter's intention. When all is true between predator and prey, an animal will remain still at the sound of the string, giving the arrow time to make its mark. But oftentimes, a crouch or leap sends the shaft harmlessly earthbound.

The sound of the string captivates the traditional archer. It is something few others understand. Traditional archers have ancestral bonds to archery no matter our race, religion, or country of origin. Somewhere, before our time, our prior people did it. That is why the sound of the string pushing a feather-fletched shaft is, to us and our forefathers all, soulful.

On Africa

I've always felt an attachment to Africa, a gravitational pull toward it, something from within guiding me to it. I thought at first that it was the animals. I think now it may be the people, some of whom I may only remember a sentence or two of a conversation as our paths crossed. Some I still speak to frequently. All of them I remember fondly. So this is my Africa, as I've known it, and as I hope to know it again. I hope my memory is true to the truth.

The Sound of the String

"I need to go to Africa."
"What is it you're looking for?"
"I'm not sure, but it's there."
"But you've never been there."
"Some part of Africa lives deep in me.
Some part of me is there."
"Will you come back?"
"I will."
"Then go."

Making Thabazimbi

The workbench has been cleared and swept clean by the old horsehair brush that hangs on the nail above it. He rolls out the butcher's paper and tapes both ends to the bench with masking tape.

A plywood form for the bow stands clamped into the vise at the front of the bench. Gordon Bradford carefully lays out all of the laminates for the new longbow he is about to build. A clear fiberglass first, followed by a western yew for the back, three laminates of bamboo for the core, another yew for the belly, and one final laminate of clear glass. A heavy riser of burled cocobolo is set to the side. It will be sandwiched into the laminates while they're being glued together.

The epoxy is measured into two small paper cups, each part exactly to the top, then combined into an old clear plastic food container, and folded slowly together like a heavy batter. The bow oven is set to one hundred eighty degrees and turned on to preheat. Gordon lifts the lid of the plywood kiln to check that all four light bulbs are burning. Wearing latex gloves and an old cotton work shirt, he begins the process of building his newest longbow named Thabazimbi. The bow is already a part of Gordon. He has seen it in his mind's eye, planned its every detail. He is building it for his first African safari.

The glue is spread over the top surface of each laminate, the excess scraped with a rubber spatula in one slow, careful movement from one end to the other without stopping. Then he begins the process of stacking one laminate onto the other and applying glue to the dry sides as they are turned upward.

"Wet on wet, no regret," he tells himself as he methodically assembles the back and core laminates, placing them onto the form. The cocobolo riser is placed on top and taped in place with white fiber packing tape. The belly laminates are placed on top of the riser fade-outs and the final clear laminates are added onto the belly. He covers the assembly with plastic wrap and lays a piece of fire hose across the top of the bow. He lifts the upper half of the form over it and bolts it to the bottom, rechecks the alignment of the limb laminates and the riser and carefully begins to fill the fire hose with air.

The lights dim in the old workshop as the air compressor kicks on, thump, thump, thump. Gordon says a silent prayer that the circuit breaker doesn't trip as he watches the hose fill to sixty pounds of pressure. The laminates are compacted together and the excess glue oozes out dripping down the sides of the form. He checks that all of the pieces of his new hunting partner are stacked tightly and their edges match. Finally, he says another prayer over the bow and passes his hands slowly over both sides, from one end to the other. He manifests the finished bow, sees it at full draw, and then prays,

"Thank you for providing me the simple pleasure of hunting the way people did when your son walked the earth."

He lifts the entire bow form and places it into the oven. He closes the lid and says, "Good luck, friend," and leaves it to bake for the next four hours.

The Flight

The plane ride is sixteen hours non-stop. Gordon sets his watch ahead six hours to South African time and sees that it's already eleven o'clock there. He decides to start living on destination time to acclimate faster.

He catches the attention of a flight attendant. "May I please have two Pinotages and a bottle of water when you have time?"

"Pleasure," she says as she walks to the food prep area.

What a beautiful, polite way to give confirmation to a request, Gordon thinks as he opens Dan Millman's <u>Body Mind Mastery</u> to page one.

She didn't say yes, sure, uh huh, she said pleasure, meaning it would be her pleasure. How polite, he thinks, and becomes happy because politeness is such a simple thing and pleasing to all involved. Being from the South, manners matter to him. Everybody, no matter who they are, deserves respect, except people who don't act respectfully in public. They deserve a boot in the rump.

The flight attendant returns with two small bottles of red wine and a bottle of water. Gordon folds down the tray table. He says, "Thank you very much, ma'am", at this she smiles because it gives her dignity to be called ma'am, and to know that her services are appreciated. He pulls a melatonin pill from his pocket and swallows it with the first small bottle of wine, drinking it all with without stopping. He drinks half of the water, and caps the bottle to save the other half until he wakes. He pours the second Pinotage into a plastic cup and sips on it as he starts to read.

Chapter One, Natural Laws. "Nature's way is simple and easy, but men prefer what is intricate and artificial." — Lao Tzu

Enough said, I already like this one, he thinks as he relates the Tzu observation to his passion for the longbow. *Hunting has become a product-driven, goal-oriented mess. Kids in America think you have to have a four-wheeler, rifle rack, range finder, fourteen scent eliminating suits (one for every possible hunting situation), twelve pairs of boots, a pop-up blind that fits over the four-wheeler, a pop-up blind to use twenty yards from the four-wheeler, a hand-held GPS, and a survival kit with fourteen days of rations in case they get lost and the neighbor's dog can't readily find them when it goes outside to relieve itself.*

Hunters in America have been duped into thinking they're not good hunters unless they buy and carry the newest gear, they can't kill a deer without the latest weapons, and they believe it. They suffer from kill anxiety, born of product overload, which is fed by continual retail therapy: If I buy more hunting products, I'll kill more animals. I didn't kill any more animals than before I bought the products. I'm not a good hunter. I need to buy more products to be better.

The more high-tech gadgets that a hunter uses the less reliant he becomes on his own natural skills. Kids are growing up thinking it is the money that you spend that makes you a better hunter, advertising tells them so, and they believe it.

Gordon has sent some articles he had written about traditional archery to editors of hunting magazines. The responses he got were that the stories were good but the only thing their readers wanted to know is what you killed, what you used to kill it with, and the stories have to be much shorter to leave space for advertisements. *What a crock of bull. Nobody wants hunting stories anymore.*

There's a whole generation of people who only want to know what products they need to buy to kill more and bigger animals.

Hunting with the longbow satisfies Gordon in a way hard for most people to understand. It's a feeling, an emotion that is not easy to explain. It doesn't matter how many kills come or how big they are, as long as you take an adult and the killing is good.

Millman would understand. Lao Tzu would, too.

He drinks the rest of the wine, puts the book in the seat pocket with the water, and gets up to use the bathroom before the effects of the alcohol and pill set in. When he reaches the bathroom a man steps out wearing jeans and a camouflage shirt and cap. As they pass each other, Gordon thinks about the man and wonders if he ever wears regular clothes or if he has to make everybody aware that he's a hunter everywhere he goes, all of the time.

Afraid there might be a springbok in row twenty-three, or warthogs in the aisle? That camo pattern won't blend in with your seat back, fella, I hope you can get to your rifle in time for the kudu near the cockpit...oh yeah, we're on a friggin' plane! I forgot, we can't hunt here, we can only read books, sleep, eat bad food, and wait to hunt after we land. We don't need our camouflage here; we won't need it until we're actually in Africa. Sometimes I just don't get people. He doesn't even have the wits to realize that by the time he reaches camp, all of the smells of the airport, the plane, the city, and the over-used bathroom he just stepped out of will be firmly impregnated into those camo clothes, and he'll wonder why the animals keep getting wind of him.

Gordon gets into the bathroom and slides the bolt to lock the door. He's surprised at how loud the crack of the steel bolt sounds inside the hard surfaced room. The camo-man left the seat up, apparently not knowing that women ride airplanes, too.

After he finishes Gordon washes his hands and face knowing he'll feel better when he wakes up if he's clean. As he dries he catches the crow's feet at the corners of his eyes and says out loud, "Well, old boy, it took forty years but you made it."

Sometimes Gordon feels older than he is, but he's felt behind schedule his entire life, always playing catch-up and never having done enough. Most of all, he misses adventure. A friend started him on books about Sir Richard Burton and he realizes how mundane the average life is. Hemingway captured Gordon and gave him travel through reading. Gordon related to Ruark well, growing up in the same region of the country. He cried openly at the end of <u>The Old Man and the Boy</u>.

Gordon didn't grow up the same as Ruark, though. He never knew a grandfather. Both of his died before he was born. Gordon's father was never an outdoorsman. Gordon took to the woods on his own. Most likely his time in the woods started from the bad marriage of his parents. He just didn't want to be home for the abuse they heaved upon each other so he took to the woods. In the woods, everything is fair. If you torment a bee's nest you get stung. If you stalk a bullfrog slowly, quietly, and then strike quick with your right hand, he's yours. If you get your fingers too close to the jaws of a snapping turtle, there's a good chance you'll lose one. Gordon tested this theory with sticks when he was eight years old and was quickly convinced. The woods are honest. Gordon likes that the most. People always come from angles, manipulate things to their advantage, argue to win instead of seeing what's right and just accepting it.

He's showing gray at the sideburns, his back seems constantly sore, but overall, he's young in his mind and heart. *You need to cut those sideburns a bit higher to hide some of that gray, man.* He cleans the sink and counter, throws away his paper towels and those of other passengers with fewer manners, and opens the door. Clack.

He settles back into his seat, leans it as far back as it will go, and then tries to push it just a bit further, wishing he could afford first class. He puts on his headphones and falls asleep thinking about kudu.

The Three Compadres

"*B*urp, waitress, beer me!" comes from behind Gordon. It rouses him into that half-asleep, annoyed state when you want sleep very badly but someone prevents you from it.

"Waitress, beer me, ha, ha, ha." The camouflage traveler and his buddies laugh amongst themselves.

Not only is Gordon annoyed at having his sleep disturbed, the rudeness toward the flight attendant really rubs him the wrong way. The flight attendant serves the beer as fast as she can because most of the plane understands that it's time to sleep, except for the camo-compadres who seem to think they can drink their way to Africa. When she gets to the men with the beer, the loud-mouthed one says, "Are we there yet?"

"No sir, we have eleven more hours until we arrive."

"Eleven more hours!"

"Yes sir."

"Well, keep the beer coming!"

All three of the buddies burst out into laughter as the waitress walks back to the food prep area. Gordon can't help but make the plane pleasant again. He stands up and walks back toward the men, and when he gets to their row he kneels down and folds his arms on the loudmouth's armrest.

"What?" says the loudmouthed one.

"Excuse me?" says Gordon, giving the man a second chance to show manners.

"What do *you* want?"

"Are you going hunting, friend?" Gordon says politely.

"Yeah, so?" the loudmouth says defensively.

"Me too," Gordon says and he sees the loudmouth soften with approval to the intrusion into his party.

"Where you going?" Gordon asks the loudmouth.

"Way up north of Pretoria, I forget the name, we found the place on the internet. They're going to pick us up in Johannesburg and drive us there."

"I'll be a little west of there in a place called Thabazimbi. You know we still have a three-to four-hour drive after we land to get that far north."

"Good deal, bud, good luck there." The loudmouth thinks he has a new compadre in Gordon, and misses the subtle advice Gordon tried to give to him that the travel wouldn't stop when the plane lands.

"Let me give you some advice," Gordon says more directly.

"What's that?"

"It's only nine-thirty east coast time so you think you can party all night, but you've already screwed up. You see, my friend, it's three-thirty in the morning in South Africa. That's why all of the other people on this plane who have a clue how to travel are trying to sleep now. Your rudeness to me, the other passengers on this plane, and the flight attendant is not acceptable. You are an embarrassment to Americans, an embarrassment to hunters, and are living proof that your parents did a poor job raising you. Now this is what's going to happen, you're going to sit here and be quiet. I'm going to go back to sleep, and if you wake me again you'll miss all of the wonderful food in Africa because you'll have a broken jaw."

At this Gordon stands and when he does the loudmouth looks as if he may make a move on him. To emphasize his stated position, Gordon puts his boot firmly onto the front of the loudmouth's seat close enough to his crotch to be serious. Gordon leans in close folding his arms across his knee, and looks the man straight in the eye.

"Look here, friend," he says, "I'm only telling you the truth. I know you want to give me a thrashing but you can't. You could jump now but you'll be down before you get up. You could jump me when I turn my back but you won't because you know if I have the stones to confront you and your two buddies, I have the stones to finish you and your two buddies. You're half in the bag already and I've kicked the crap out of better men than you when they were sober. So what you're going to do now is sit here, finish your beer quietly, and think about what I've told you."

At this Gordon looks right to make sure the two buddies are paying attention, and they are. They look sheepishly at Gordon like they're already getting their butts kicked. Metaphorically, they are.

"So this is what happens now, I'm going back to my seat to sleep. I strongly suggest the next time you interact with the flight attendants you treat them with the respect they deserve. Their job is difficult enough without having to deal with half-wit, rednecks like you.

"Two more things I want you to remember. First, my name is Gordon Bradford. Secondly, my suggestion to you is, if you care about hunting at all, you need to start representing it in a more adult, positive manner, because we're losing, my friend, and jerks like you aren't helping our cause at all."

At this he removes his boot from the loudmouth's seat, stands straight, turns his back to him, and returns to his seat. He never looks back because he knows nothing is going to happen.

He sits back and closes his eyes again to sleep. A minute later he feels the flight attendant's hand on his shoulder and she bends to whisper in his ear, "Thank you."

"Pleasure," is all he says without opening his eyes. He drifts off to sleep again feeling that he's already been touched by Africa and, in some small way, touched it too.

At one a.m. (seven South African time) Gordon awakens. Stiff from neck to ankles, he stretches as much as possible in his seat and then stands in the aisle to stretch completely. He grabs his empty wine bottles, finishes the water, and walks to the food prep area to throw away his trash. The flight attendants, neither of whom he knows, look up from their newspapers. They've already convicted him of being an irritant. He just smiles and walks to the trash. A flight attendant gets up to help and Gordon says, "Sit, please. I can help myself, you'll have enough to do when the others wake up." She smiles and without a word sits and returns to her reading, not sure if she's comfortable with him or not. She keeps one eye on the paper and one on Gordon. Everyone is asleep except a few lone readers and T.V. watchers. As he walks he notices how loud the plane is when you're the lone walker of the aisles and you have seven and a half more hours until you land.

He returns to his seat, picks up his book but can't read in the dimly lit cabin. He doesn't want to turn his reading light on for fear he'll disturb the other passengers. He slips on his headphones, turns on a music channel, and soon is asleep again with his head on a rolled-up airline blanket.

Dreaming of a lone kudu that steps out of the bush and silently walks to the water Gordon readies for the shot. Turbulence shakes the plane and his head bobs just enough to wake him from his dream. *Dang it, I was almost there.* He takes off his headphones and the noise of the plane, once again, drones in his head.

He stirs to his feet and checks his watch, three-thirty a.m., five more hours until the plane lands. He asks the flight attendants about breakfast and they assure him it's coming soon so he uses the bathroom one more time, amazed at the mess left by the other passengers. *I wonder what their homes are like?* He thinks. He picks up some of the mess that looks as if it may be disease free and leaves the rest for the folks with the rubber gloves to get when the plane lands. He washes his hands and face, and goes to his seat to find that breakfast is being served. He opts for fruit, yogurt, and muesli to keep himself feeling light and his intestines moving and has coffee and two more waters. After the trays are cleared, he picks up the Millman book and reads until the plane begins to descend into Johannesburg.

The plane lands and taxies to the airport without event. The passengers all stand and it seems ten different languages erupt as wives snap commands at husbands to get the carry-ons down and husbands snap back impatiently at the impatience of their wives. The plane takes on the feeling of an open-air market with chatter, bartering, and hand gestures. Everyone wants off, but the plane hasn't docked yet. Gordon chuckles at the scene, relaxed that they are on the ground, and secure that one of the most difficult parts of his adventure is over. As he exits the plane, the flight attendant says, "Enjoy our country."

When he gets off of the plane, the first thing he does is hold his nostrils closed and blows to pop his eardrums clear. The final descent left him feeling like his ears were inside out.

The three compadres are standing in the terminal looking hung-over. Gordon thinks about them paying now for their earlier indiscretions,

Sin when you're drunk, pay when you're sober.

Gordon walks by and looks the big one in the eye as he passes, trying to get a feel for the odds of getting his butt kicked. Their eyes meet but there's no reaction on either side, so Gordon walks on without a break in his stride.

"Bradford," the big one shouts.

The muscles at the base of Gordon's skull tighten and his shoulders tense. He doesn't want this on his first day. He turns and walks back to the group wondering how much time he'll miss if he gets thrown in jail and how much the bail and bribes will be. Will he be able to get out of jail and get to camp in time for a few days in the kudu blinds? Luckily, the big one is right handed, his luggage is on the ground beside his right leg leaving his left knee exposed. Gordon prepares to take the big one's knee out before throwing uppercuts to the jaws of the other two. Uppercuts usually catch the occasional brawler off guard. He looks the big one in the eye and preplans his foot folding the man's left knee sideways.

"Yes, friend, what can I do for you?" Gordon asks.

"Listen, Bradford, uh, you were right. All that stuff you said about representing hunters poorly and stuff. Well, you were right. It made me think about how fragile hunting is and how easy it is to screw it up for everyone and, well, you were right."

"Thanks, friend, I'm glad to hear you say that. I was really expecting to get my butt kicked."

At that the four chuckle and they all shake hands and bid each other good luck.

Gordon walks alone to the baggage claim. On his way he passes the flight attendant who's been watching the confrontation with the three compadres. Their eyes meet and he pretends to wipe sweat from his brow. She laughs at the gesture and they both nod as if to say, "Pleasure."

With the bow case secured and the duffle on his shoulder Gordon makes his way to a roped area where families are reuniting, drivers are meeting passengers, and PHs are meeting clients. He sees the sign for Thabazimbi Bush Adventures and a man behind it in khakis. He knows he is finally home, in Africa.

Meeting Lucas and Moses

"Mr. VanZandt?"

"Mr. Bradford?"

"I'd rather you call me Gordon."

"Then Gordon it will be."

"My name is Lucas, I work for Mr. VanZandt, and I'll be your PH for this trip and hopefully many more."

They both smile and shake hands vigorously and Lucas talks in Afrikaans to an older black man with him. The old man reaches for Gordon's bag but Gordon refuses. The old man insists on at least taking one and Gordon obliges, not wanting to offend him.

"What's your name, sir?"

"Moses, Mr. Gordon."

"Please just call me Gordon."

"As you wish, Gordon."

The old man looks at Gordon to be sure calling him by his first name is the correct thing to do and smiles his approval.

"Really, Moses, Gordon is my name, Mr. was my father." He reaches to shake the old man's hand and holds it firmly, feeling the pulse of his heart through the thin, aged skin of his palm. The heartbeat brings to Gordon's mind the sound of African drums, and he feels like he's holding onto Africa itself. Moses looks Gordon in the eye, searching for any signs of bad intention but finds none. Then Moses smiles and they walk like friends through the airport and load the luggage into Lucas' Land Rover. All of them are glad to rid themselves of the formalities.

"I've never seen a Rover pickup, Lucas, this is great."

"It's bushveld standard, Gordon, a bakkie. These Rovers are great utility vehicles if you get them stripped of all the bells and whistles. A small diesel engine, a rugged chassis, and a rock-solid transfer case and drive train are all that's required in the bush. Some guys run Toyotas, Nissans, Mazdas or the like in the bush, but for me, I hope I can drive a Rover as long as I can hunt."

Moses opens the front passenger door for Gordon but Gordon refuses the offer and says,

"Please, Moses, I'd feel better if you would ride up front."

"But Gordon, sir, you are our guest, it would not be right to put you in the back."

"Moses, please, I'd rather be here in the back. I appreciate your kindness but I don't want to be pampered, coddled or fawned over. I just want to experience this place as ordinarily as I can. I want to work with you, hunt with you, learn from you and about you. That's the experience I want. Besides, Moses, if I fall asleep, it will be better in the back."

"As you wish...Gordon."

The three men get in the bakkie and the little diesel finds the highway. Gordon sits in the middle of the rear seat leaning forward between the two in front so he can see and hear everything. As Gordon looks into the old black man's eyes, he notices a tear in each, holding steady to the inside corners. He imagines the life behind the man's eyes, living hard, working hard, and struggling just to be good. In a country with so many poor, it would be easy for a man to join the campaign of the wrong doers. Gordon imagines the narrow path in Africa that Moses has chosen, and he has to ask.

"Moses, I'm sure I'll get to know Lucas in the blinds, but could you tell me about yourself, what your job is, and how you got here? I'm interested."

How Moses Met VanZandt

$\mathcal{M}$oses' father joined the Christian faith when the missionaries were building a nearby church. They offered work when there wasn't any and hadn't been for a long time. The work was coupled with daily disquisitions on Christianity and by the end of the build most of the local laborers were converts with slightly heavier pockets and greatly enriched souls.

The thing Moses' father liked most about that time in his life was that for once he and his people felt as though they were not forgotten. They had work. They were building something good in their community, they were building families, and the village had a sense of community not before realized. The missionaries seemed trustworthy, honest, and genuinely kind. The racial tension building in South Africa at the time seemed to be absent in their small community, at least temporarily.

It was the beginning of apartheid. Communities were being separated and segregated from each other, sometimes by force. The Afrikaner-controlled government decided to make racism its legal policy rather than just the mindset of its members.

Moses grew up with the teachings of Christ in his parents' home. He grew to take the religion, the demeanor, and the optimistic conviction of his father. He learned at an early age that what is right is not always easy, but it is still right. Doing what is right rests lightly on your conscience, and easily inside of you. When you feel good inside, it makes your outside circumstances easier to bear.

When Moses finished school his father gave him the most important thing he could, freedom. The family Bible with the tattered black leather binding was handed ceremoniously from father to son. Inside the cover was cash, not much, but more than Moses had ever seen at one time.

"Father, I can't take this from you."

"Moses, I want you to have them both, I want you to start your own life. I will ask you, son, only one thing: Never forget your past."

"My past is who I am, you, mother, the church, and the school. I am all of those things."

"This country is changing, son. I've been praying for the right path to be found by you. You have to find your way now, and I have business to attend to in the city."

"What work, father? I can go with you."

"This is not labor son, this is resistance."

"I don't understand."

"You will, son, keep reading, read everything you can, and you will understand.

"Moses, please understand that I'm not kicking you out of my home, I'm not getting rid of you. I'm just asking you to fly. I want you to have a better life than I. I want you to work hard, continue to read, study, and some day I want you to be free."

The next day Moses gathered his clothing, his Bible, and his money. He kissed his crying mother, said goodbye to his little sisters, and walked out of the only home he had ever known. He walked down a sandy, red-clay road toward the only town he had ever seen in his life.

He needed to find work and a place to live. He could live out-side for a while. He'd slept outside many times and it didn't bother him at all. He had to find work though, as he was taught the value of money and didn't want to waste the gift his father had given him. He had to do what his father had told him, find his own way.

Night fell on his second night walking as a truck drove toward him from behind. He didn't turn to look, and he didn't gesture for a ride. He just walked. His mind was heavy, laden with fear, confusion, questions, and a complete lack for the answers.

The driver of the truck, a young sandy-haired professional hunter named VanZandt, saw someone in the road carrying a small sack and wondered what he was doing. A white man at that time would not normally stop to pick up a black man, but he saw it was just a kid. He pulled the truck over on the otherwise empty highway.

"Hey, kid."

"Yes, sir."

"What are you doing out here in the middle of the night?"

"I'm walking to the city to find work and a place to live."

"You can't go to the city, you'll be turned away without a work permit."

"Why, sir, do you say that?"

"Because you're black and South Africa passed the law of apartheid. It's separating all of the races from each other."

"But why?"

"The old Boers and the Afrikaners, whites, you know, they think it's better that way. It's better for them anyway."

"But what about you, sir?"

"I'm just a hunter, I don't care for politics or politicians. As long as they let me book clients and find game for them to shoot, and I pay my taxes to them for the privilege, we're both happy. Get in."

As they drove, Moses became more worried about his situation. Was this some kind of test from his father? Was it cruelty or a joke? What would he do if he was denied access to the city and couldn't find work? He remembered his father telling him to read and in desperation he saw the hunter's folded newspaper on the seat.

"May I read your newspaper, sir?"

"You can read?"

"Yes sir, very well."

The hunter saw the nervous agitation in the young man and thought that if the reading helped, it was a small request to give for a young man lost in a country now turning against him.

"Use the flashlight there."

Moses picked up the paper and began to read.

"It's new today."

"Thank you, sir." He read on, desperately searching to find a way out of his situation. He read so fast that the meanings of the words were lost and the sentences became strands of single words.

He found an article about a group of black men belonging to the African National Congress (ANC), and slowed down to pay attention because his father had spoken of this group. The article was about the ANC forming a planning council to join with other groups and races to discuss changes in the new government and how to maintain their rights as citizens of South Africa.

As he read he found that the men were detained by police and after questioning brought back to their homes and placed under house arrest for committing acts of treason against the new government. At the end of the article there was a published list of names and as Moses read, he found the name of his own father. The reason he was told to leave became apparent to him. Hyperactive thoughts crossed his mind. Should he tell of his father's arrest, should he hide it, should he go back home, will he be detained himself because of his father's action, can he hide his identity?

"Sir," he says politely. "What do you think of this apartheid?"

"I only know what goes on in the bushveld, kid. There, everyone — black or white — has a role. Everyone does their part to contribute to the camp, working as a team. My cook is a very valuable asset in camp and he's black. My trackers are irreplaceable and they're black. The hunters come from around the world and bring money to all of us and they're usually white except for the occasional aristocrat from India or the Middle East. If we all do our jobs, no one gets hurt and everyone gets paid. If one of us gets hurt, everyone helps, because a man down in camp makes the whole lot of us weaker. I don't know what goes on in the city but I do know they would all appreciate each other more if they had to stand a buffalo charge together. In the bush, bonds are built between men that people in the city will never understand. A man can't be judged by where he was born, his color, or even his family. All of us are born good, and at some point we make our own decision to stay that way or not."

Moses imagined the safety of a hunting camp, out in the bush, away from the city and the police, a respite from his current turmoil. He saw a co-op of sorts — pleasing the client, the common goal of all.

"I think apartheid is a bad thing," Moses said quietly, unsure of himself.

"I'm sure you do, kid, I'm sure you do," the hunter says, not offering his own opinion.

The two drove in silence while they pondered just what to do about the other. After an hour of silent worry and prayer, Moses decided to take a risk and show faith in this hunter who's already shown him one kindness.

"Sir," he says softly.

"Yes?"

"I read in your newspaper some men who were members of the ANC have been put into house arrest for conspiracy and for entering the city without permission."

"Yes."

"One of those men was my father."

"Really?"

"He told me to leave his house two days ago. I don't know what to do. I don't know if my father knew there was trouble coming or if he just thought it was time for me to leave. I don't know if I should go home or continue to the city, sir, what should I do?"

"If you go to the city you'll be turned away. If you go home you could be accused of conspiracy because of your father. If you stay on the streets you'll become a victim or a criminal."

"I won't be a criminal."

"An empty stomach makes a man do things he wouldn't normally do, kid. An empty stomach is a powerful force."

"I have faith that God will provide an answer for me. I won't need to steal."

"What can you do?"

"I can do anything, I read very well. I am young, but I can learn any job in a hunting camp." His mouth had gotten ahead of his thoughts and he was caught, intentions exposed.

VanZandt decides an informal interview is necessary, partly out of curiosity, mostly to teach the young man how much he doesn't know.

"Can you read spoor?"

"No, sir."

"Can you eviscerate an animal, skin it or butcher it?"

"No, sir." Moses didn't like the way his first job interview was going.

"Can you cook?"

"No, sir, but I can learn."

"Can you clean rifles?"

"I've never seen a rifle, except in books."

"Can you hold your urine for hours in a leopard blind waiting for the killer to appear? Not release it until after the shots are fired, the leopard charges, and then runs into the bush to escape the volley of bullets sent toward him by a client who has released his own urine? Then, act as if it's normal for a grown man with a rifle to wet his pants?"

"That sounds exciting, sir, very exciting. Is that how we make a living?" Already confident that he was the man for the job, Moses continued to speak. "I can hold my water for hours, my teachers in school were very strict and would not let us leave the classroom until they decided it was time. I see now that it was solid training."

"So you have good bladder control. That is an asset in a hunting camp. What other skills do you have?"

Moses racked his brain for another valuable skill, but he was just a boy trying to be a man. All he knew how to do was read well and help his parents. His thoughts came slowly but coalesced and he began to itemize his value.

"I can gather firewood and water, I can clean anything inside or outside, I can smoke a bees' nest and gather honey, I can do laundry, and because I can read I can learn to do anything else. I am young, my legs and back are strong. I can carry things for the older men, and I can run fast and far if you need me to."

The hunter gathered his thoughts. He saw the desperation in the boy. He pondered about his camp and the need, or lack of need, for a boy like this.

It couldn't hurt to give him a try, he thought, *at least I can keep him out of trouble for a while.*

"Well, kid, I have never seen a young man with no hunting camp skills at all so full of confidence."

Moses wondered if his desperation showed. It did.

"I like your confidence, kid. If you give my camp a chance, work hard for me and learn, I'll give you a try for a while."

That was five decades ago. Moses proved a valuable asset to the camp and never left. VanZandt's hunting operation grew and Moses to this day is considered an integral part. Moses still worries though; it's just what he does.

In the early days he sent money home to help care for his parents and his sisters. He didn't need much for himself because VanZandt provided his food, lodging, and let him keep his tips from the clients.

Three years went by and Moses had learned nearly every job in the camp. He was happy every morning and went to sleep every evening with the contentment that a satisfying day gives a soul. Then came a letter from his family. While traveling to an ANC meeting his father had been killed. It was an automobile accident on a rural road with no witnesses and no one close enough to help. All of the occupants in the vehicle were found dead at the scene of the accident, no further explanation was reported. Moses needed none. He knew the cause of his father's death. He learned that a political agenda has no regard for family or peripheral damage. He thinks of the goodness of his father and remembers him every day.

Samuel

*M*oses continued to send money to his mother until she died of a broken heart. This firmly convinced him that life in the bush was better than life outside of it.

As the decades passed Moses and VanZandt grew to respect and consider one another family. The old PH watched as Moses married and began his own family. Moses, just like his father, had one son. He named his son Samuel. He raised him as he was raised, to learn, to read, and to work hard and honestly. When the time came for Moses' son to leave school, VanZandt made Moses an offer.

"Hey, Mo."

"Yes, Mr. Van."

"Your boy is a smart one, isn't he? What I mean to say is, he's a lot like you."

"Thank you, sir, I'm very proud of him."

"You know, Mo, I am too. Listen, I want to discuss something with you."

Thinking there was another job offer being made, Moses starts contemplating the benefits of having his only son work by his side. He pictures the two of them hunting, tracking, and making the best, most professional hunting camp in Africa. What a thrill to have the time as men that he and his father were never able to share. What a life opportunity for both of them.

"He would be an asset to the camps sir."

"I know he would, Mo, but I'm afraid he'd be so good he'd take your job."

"He may, then I'd be on the street again, just like when you found me."

They both laugh, think, and the silence becomes awkward. Moses, as he did years ago, trudges headfirst into the unknown.

"What are you thinking, Mr. Van?"

"Moses, he's a smart young man. You and I both know that he's too smart to hang around a hunting camp and work his tail off like us his entire life."

"But we're getting old too, Mr. Van, we may need some fresh legs soon."

"Moses, we'll be all right. We've done this long enough. We wouldn't know what to do with ourselves if we slowed down. We just have to work a little smarter, help will find us when we need it, it always has."

"God provides, sir."

"He always does. So I want to send your son to university. He'll have a real chance for a better life if we can get him through."

"Sir, how can it happen?"

"Listen, Mo, there are just a few blacks being let into Wits University in Johannesburg. I know it's a stretch and I'm not pretending it's going to be easy for any of us. If we all get on this together, I think we can get him in and get him out with an engineering degree."

"But I could never afford that, and the government won't subsidize a black man."

"Look, Mo, you let me worry about the tuition, you worry about the books and food, and tell Samuel to work his hind quarters off for four years because once he gets in they'll look for anything, any excuse to kick him out. He's got to understand that he's a target; he'll be tested every day. If he gets through this, he'll have opportunity the likes that you and I have never seen. Moses, talk to him about your father, about the resistance, and about the end of apartheid. It's coming, Mo. Don't you want him ready to take advantage of that?"

"Of course I do, even if I never see it."

"Either way, Mo, I feel like I owe this to you. We've been through so much together. We started as a young PH and a camp helper with one camp. Now we run multiple concessions together and have other PHs working for us. We've done a lot."

"Working for you, Mr. Van."

"Come on, Mo, everyone knows I can't do anything without you."

"That's very generous of you to say sir, but you're a prolific liar."

"Moses, you're my right hand. You've been my tracker, my cook, my gun bearer, my driver, and you've managed to help me keep all of my body parts. Through run-ins with elephants, rhinos, leopards, lions, buffalos, snakes, spiders, and everything that's wanted a piece of me in the bush you've been there for me, unwavering."

"You were there for me when I needed you too, Mr. Van."

"I was the lucky one in that deal Moses. Listen, I can't make your boy rich, but I can give him opportunity. We can give him opportunity, but he's got to understand that it won't work unless he's fully vested in it."

The three of them drove to the University of Witwatersrand over and over again. Van and Moses sat in hallways and dean's offices while Samuel endured exams, interviews, and insults of the faculty whose job it was to prove that he was incapable of college. With each trip the three of them became more determined to prove that they and Samuel, could and would do this. Each time they left the university Samuel would fall asleep in the car like a small child, exhausted from the stress of having to prove himself every minute while on campus.

On a particularly long visit, VanZandt walked the halls like an expectant father to pass the time. He stopped near the classrooms in the school of mining engineering to look at the black and white, poster-sized photographs on the walls. He looked closely at the men in the photos, their lives being spent in deep, dark holes in the earth, bending at the waist or on their knees for hours unending. He says out loud, "How can a man work where there is no sun?"

"Quite simple," a voice from behind says to him.

"Excuse me," Van says politely, "I didn't realize you were there."

"Not a problem, sir, but will you allow me to explain?"

"Explain what?"

"How a man can work where there is no sun."

"Listen, I didn't mean to offend you."

"None taken, my good man. It's simple though — electricity."

"What?" Van thinks the man is making fun of him with the overly simplistic answer.

"First we used torches and candles, then we used oil lamps, and now we run electricity right down the bloody shaft. Man, what a difference it makes."

"What I was trying to say was, I just couldn't stand not being able to see the sun all day. I usually see it rise every morning and see it set every evening. I spend just about the entire day, every day, in it. I can't imagine what it would be like not to have it over my shoulder."

"What is it that you do, sir, if I may ask?"

"I am a professional hunter, and since we're here, allow me to introduce myself. VanZandt is my name, but Van is what I go by."

"I'm Professor Lawson, I run the Mining Engineering program here at Wits."

"Listen, professor, I didn't mean to offend you."

"Not at all, man. In fact, who in their right mind wouldn't want to be a PH? What man who has any inclination to be in the bush wouldn't give everything he has to make a living there? In the bush, every day is different from the last. Here at the university there is structure and planning in such copious amounts that a professor knows exactly what he's doing from day to day, year after year. It's wonderful in its pay and stability, but I'm afraid it does lack adventure."

The two men talk and walk the halls for an hour finding that, on the surface, they have nothing in common, but they do share an interest in the other's vocation. The professor carries on about the intricacies of mining, whether for diamonds or other resources. The engineering that goes into making a modern mine safe, efficient, and productive fascinates Van who, until now, has never given mining a second thought.

Van answers the professor's questions about hunting and tells a few stories about some of the close calls he's had in the bush, accentuating the drama. Van is a good storyteller, and rapidly develops the professor's interest in hunting into a commitment to go hunting. Then he closes the deal.

The arrangements are made for Professor Lawson to go on his first safari. He'll go deep into the bushveld with Moses and Van and hunt plains game to his heart's content. Like other professors, he'll have trophies for his office and stories to tell at the faculty lounge. Above all, he'll have adventure in his life. All of this he gained from a simple conversation started in an empty hallway with a man he didn't know.

In exchange, Van accepts only one thing from the professor. Van trades a waterbuck, a kudu, an impala, as many warthogs and partridges as the professor can shoot, and maybe a leopard, if the blood of the antelope carcasses is carried on the wind correctly. He trades all of this to the professor for a single sheet of stationary embossed with the professor's letterhead.

On the stationary, the professor will write a letter to the dean of Witwatersrand University. The letter will recommend the admission of a hardworking young man who, despite being born and raised in the bush, and being the wrong color for South Africa's current state, simply deserves a chance at success. For Van, Moses, and Samuel, the admission process to Wits University is complete.

Samuel's work ethic and ability to comprehend the intricacies of engineering earned him a bachelor's degree in three years. What would have been his fourth and final year at Wits University was spent as a junior engineer working for a major diamond mine. Like Moses, Samuel thinks of the goodness of his father every day.

The stories went on for what seemed hours, and by the end Gordon felt he knew Moses as a friend.

"Thank you, Moses, for sharing that with me."

"Pleasure, sir."

"Please, it's Gordon."

"Habit of mine, Gordon."

"I have no doubt, Moses, but I would prefer Gordon, if you don't mind."

"Pleasure, Gordon."

At this Gordon lies down in the back of the Rover and lets the whine of the tires sing him to sleep.

He wakes to the sight of a stone lodge with a heavy thatch roof, a boma, food, and drinks awaiting him. It was just like he remembered…or imagined. There is also a woman, Lucas' wife. Her name is Lise, and she is beautiful in her plainness. Khaki pants, a pullover fleece, and small ostrich skin PH boots make her look like the classic African huntress but with a more modern finish. Her blond hair is pulled through the adjusting strap of a faded cotton baseball cap that sits tight over the rest. As she turns to look at the new arrival, Gordon sees a ribbon of sun-bleached hair that has escaped the ball cap and fallen over one blue-green eye. He looks at her and she at him and they both realize they have spent more than an appropriate time on the other, so they resume their business. But they remember the moment.

Mo's Advice

*G*ordon is up before anyone else in camp except for the man who makes the coffee and tea, but it's his duty to be up first. Gordon helps himself to a mug from the kitchen and pours the coffee. He says good morning to the man in the kitchen and his greeting is returned but not much more. The man is too busy to talk, getting the breakfast ready. He's also uncomfortable because a guest has come for coffee before he has it prepared and served at the boma.

Gordon decides to sit in the dark with his coffee, smell the air, and listen to the sounds of the bush. It's his first morning at the lodge and mostly what he wants to do is just find where he fits in. The coffee is good. He inhales its thick steam and then swallows a mouthful, warming his chest as it goes. He sits alone by the embers of last night's fire and thinks about the day, the country beyond camp he hasn't seen, and the hunting he's about to experience. Most of all he just quietly thanks God for the opportunity of this experience, however it turns out. He is thankful just to be here.

"Mr. Gordon."

"Hey, Moses, how are you this morning?"

"I am well, Mr. Gordon, and you? How is the coffee?"

"Moses, your man in the kitchen makes fine coffee, please tell him I said so."

"I will, Mr. Gordon, I'm glad you're pleased."

"Moses, you seem worried. Can I help you with anything?"

"No, Mr. Gordon."

"Please call me Gordon."

"Gordon, I just worry for my camp and my hunters. I think the rains are coming and the hunting may be no good this week. If that happens there will be anger in the hunters and it will get turned toward the staff."

"Anger? I don't understand, Moses. Why would someone blame you for the weather? You can't help the weather any more than I can."

"But a man returning from the bush empty-handed often blames others for his misfortunes. As the week continues, the frustration grows, and instead of seeing the promise of the next day, he sees only the failures of the last, time that is running out, and when time is running out it creates stress on everyone."

"I'll bet you've seen it all, haven't you, Moses?"

"I've seen a good bit of good and more bad than I had ever thought possible. I've watched children perform brilliantly under pressure and turn into men right before my eyes, and I've seen too often failure turn a grown man into a scared little boy."

"What do you see for this week?"

"I don't predict the future, I take only what God gives, and I try to work with it the best I can. I can tell you, though, how I would approach a week like the one you have in front of you, Gordon."

"Please, Moses."

"Your heart and mind may betray each other to set your direction. In doing so, they may betray you. Leave your ego in camp."

"I'm not sure I understand, Moses."

"Gordon, this is not the week to wait for record book animals. Take an adult and be happy that you did, a decent representative of the species if you see one. It will be used and shared by all and its life will be celebrated. Do not wait for the champions; they may outlast your hunting time. If the rains come, you may see nothing at all. Be thankful for what you do see."

"Moses, I already am."

"But you've only seen me, Mr. Lucas, and Mrs. Lise."

"I know, Moses, I know."

The Hide

After breakfast, Lucas drops Gordon at a ground blind for the day. The walls are rough stone, hastily laid, with mortar squeezing out of the joints, never cleaned by its mason. It has a thatch roof to keep the sun off the guests who don't normally spend all day with it, and to keep the hide from acting as a chimney, wafting human scent throughout the bushveld on the subtle breezes. Lucas goes in first to check for snakes, and then pulls Gordon's gear into the blind. Gordon steps down into the blind and tests it for clearance enough to draw, point, and shoot his longbow.

"You need to make yourself comfortable, Gordon. You'll be here all day unless you radio me to take you back to camp," Lucas explains as he leaves a bottle of water and some lunch.

"Thanks, Lucas."

"Here's your radio. We'll have constant contact, but the camp is a little short handed so I'm going to have to leave you to help some of the other clients."

"Not a problem, Lucas, I'll enjoy the solitude."

"Hopefully you won't be alone for long."

Gordon unpacks, puts on some face paint, nocks an arrow and settles in. Lucas grins because he's never seen a hunter use face paint. He keeps his thoughts his own, as he doesn't yet know Gordon well enough to tease him. He leaves without saying a word.

Anticipation

irst-day anticipation causes Gordon's mind to create scenes of animals walking in on the game trails surrounding the blind. They approach slow, silent, and cautious. He sees kudu cows in the bush and carefully raises the binoculars to realize they're just Y shaped branches. He was sure he had seen faces and ears. He sees warthogs across a game trail but the binoculars reveal just rocks and termite mounds. He's positive they were moving. The shadows made them real in his imagination, his heart wanting to see them so badly it betrays him. Gordon is amused by the power of his own imagination. *You need to settle down, son, we've only been here half an hour*, he thinks. But it happens everywhere he travels and everywhere he hunts, the active imagination and the introspective discourse.

He's been shooting well but has more confidence in the bow, Thabazimbi, than he has in himself. Gordon has always been vulnerable to self-doubt.

Lucas watched at the practice butt in the morning. He commented how quiet the longbow is when it shoots.

"It's just the sound of the string, that's all. No cables, no cams, nothing mechanical, just *fffit* and it's done."

"That's all it is, Lucas, simple, quiet, and feeding mankind for thousands of years. It's organic hunting."

The Shuffle

$\mathcal{B}$ehind the blind and out of Gordon's sight, there is a small interplay of bushveld animals. They all want the same thing, water, but are afraid of the danger that comes when one is prone to thirst. There are guinea fowl, warthogs, kudu, and wildebeest all urging the other to go first. It's an amalgamation of beasts in a chaotic but centuries-old performance that hunters rarely see.

Get out there, a warthog urges the guineas, snorting and coughing from the dust that fills its sinuses.

The wildebeests work through the crowd, hoping to get a kudu bumped into the open.

Knock a kudu loose and get one out to the water, kudus always get shot. If there's a hunter in there we'll know.

The kudu all hold firm to their herd but are pressed forward, their long legs invade the space of the warthogs.

Let the hogs go, says a kudu. *There are plenty of them.*

The hogs snort and squeal, and then turn on the kudu pushing them back.

39

Back off before you get a tusk to the foreleg! Just send the guineas and be done with it, says the largest and most irascible warthog, and with that the pigs turn again and charge the guineas.

Wrack, wrack, wraaaack, the guineas erupt and reluctantly half fly and half run to the water hole. Heads bobbing and eyes searching, they find nothing in the blind so they settle at the edge of the water and begin to drink.

Inside the blind it's quiet except for the sounds of guinea fowl scratching about. Gordon has no idea there's a dance recital happening behind him. Three fowl line up at the water directly away from Gordon. He can't help thinking about shooting all three with one arrow, shish kabob-style, to bring to Lise to cook for dinner.

Earlier, he asked Lucas about shooting them for camp meat and Lucas shared his favorite guinea fowl recipe. He said that you take three guineas and place them in a large pot of boiling water with a rock. Add salt, pepper, spices and boil it all for twenty minutes. Then you remove the guinea fowl, throw them away, and eat the rock. Gordon smiles as he thinks about the joke that must have been told a thousand times by Lucas, and thousands more by VanZandt before him. How old things are new to strangers, and how strangers laugh just to be polite. He elected not to shoot guineas.

It is fun thinking of drilling three with one arrow, though, he reflects. Lucas did say that some of the trackers would eat them if he really wanted to shoot one but he remembers the advice of Moses and decides to wait for the kudu.

The wildebeests know that a hunter won't shoot a guinea fowl unless he is terribly bored, or has shot all of the animals he can afford. They decide to make a wide circle and come in far in front of the blind checking the shooting holes as they go.

Gordon looks out of the shooting window to see a wildebeest standing at sixty yards staring directly into the hide. He leans left to get more view to the right and sees the rest of the herd. There are several young bulls in the front. With them are a few large bulls with horns past their ears and heavy bosses meeting close at the center of their heads.

The large bulls cautiously wait at the periphery as the young wildebeests work their way toward the water. In some eternally rehearsed sacrifice, the old bulls wait for signs of trouble, sending the non-breeders in first. Eventually, they all file in.

The wildebeests shuffle, constantly testing the wind and peering into the shooting hole. Their leg muscles spasm nervously, readying to spring back at any sign of danger. Their nerves incite Gordon's nerves. His heart pounds as he tries to slow his breathing and regain calm.

Seeing the wildebeest get their water unharmed, the kudu become resentful that they waited.

Let's go, says a young cow, mature in body but still adolescent in mind.

Patience, an older bull cautions. *We've come this far, we can wait. You can see the water, don't let your thirst betray you.*

The warthogs take to rolling in the dirt to pass the time and let something else get killed rather than them. The dominant kudu bull chooses a bull, younger than himself but one he knows will challenge him in the future. He urges the lesser bull forward.

Go, it's your turn to lead the herd in.

The younger bull fills with pride, not knowing that the older bulls intentions were less than honorable. He walks toward the water, unknowingly double-crossed.

Gordon has resolved to shoot a wildebeest if they calm down but his plan changes abruptly as the kudu bull walks in from the left side of the blind. He doesn't notice the kudu until it's just a few steps from the water. The bull walks directly to the water and takes the front position between the wildebeests and the hide. Gordon's heart races again, thumping like the old air compressor in the workshop.

He's been dreaming of kudu for a year since the hunt was booked, now it's here. The bull is not huge but a good representative of his species, like Moses said. Sporting horns of almost two curls and ivory tips, Gordon is happy to have it standing broadside on the first day of his first safari.

With all of the fevered, trembling confidence he can harness, he slides out of the seat close to the ground. With great caution he raises Thabazimbi and himself into the dark shadows at the back of the blind. He stands to the side of the shooting hole where the kudu's vision is impaired. Watching, he tries to control his heavy breathing, and to find just the right spot above the bull's foreleg to put his arrow. He waits for the kudu and his pounding heart to relax but neither will. He steps carefully forward with his left leg, finds a spot on the canvas of the kudu's ribcage, and comes to full draw. The wildebeests no longer exist in his mind's eye, only the kudu. His heart pounds in his chest and ears. He hears, *just don't miss* inside himself and tries desperately to ignore the thought. He takes one last breath, and releases the string. Crack! The bow makes a sound that instantly tells Gordon that something has gone very, very wrong.

All Hooves Exit

*G*ordon is sick as he watches a feeble arrow pass through the tall hair on the hump above the kudu's shoulder, well above anything vital. All hooves exit the water hole in a great panic as his mind's focus expands to see the full scene of wildebeests leaping into and through the water, over each other, and through the bush, all clouded in the red dust of Africa. He watches from the small window as his kudu runs alone and out of sight. He knows the kudu won't be recovered. Instantly emotionally drained, he recreates the disaster inside the blind.

Sitting in the dark shadows he begins to pray. He prays himself into that deep-minded place where real thoughtful prayer happens. He prays the kudu does not suffer. In Gordon's mind, he and the kudu begin a spiritual dialogue.

I may die, but it won't be today. My body and my horns may be found, but it won't be by you.

Gordon prays to remember the curls, the chip off the left tip, and the little bit of ivory at the ends.

I am too far ahead for even your dogs to catch. Some days the predators win, some days the prey escape. That is life in Africa. It never changes, regardless of the outcome. The lessons of the bushveld remain the same.

Gordon refuses to talk back to the kudu, only prays with more concentration to hear, to see, and to feel anything that will help his despair.

Deflated from the message and the confirmation of what he had already thought, he begins to look inside himself for the answer to what went wrong. He finds his heart and asks, *Why were you so scared, beating out of my chest?*

The heart answers, *Hearts always fear failure, that's what they do best.*

When you do that, it's hard to think, he scolds the heart, *and why say just don't miss when I'm trying to shoot?*

I was scared.

Then his mind speaks up and says, *Listen to your mind during the times intense thought is needed, and failures will be few. Minds only look for solutions and think positively. They don't fear failure. They only find the path to success. That is what minds do best, they find the answer.*

Why didn't you help me? Gordon asks his mind. *You saw what was happening and you let me fail.*

I was there, trying to be heard, but the heart had taken your attention. The pounding in your chest and your ears was so great it left no voice for mindful thought. The heart drowned me. Listen for me next time. Ask for me. Save your heart for the celebration. That is what hearts do best.

Gordon opens his eyes sorry he was not mindful of his mind but grateful they talked and thankful his mind was willing to lead the next time they shoot the bow together.

He holds Thabazimbi across his lap and examines it from tip to tip. He finds that the lower limb of the bow had struck the rock ledge inside the blind. He had stepped too close to the shooting hole. There was a small fracture in the clear glass of the lower limb and a hole in his heart. The heart had done exactly what it feared the most, failed. Now for Gordon, there was a dilemma.

He waits to make sure all of the animals are gone then leaves the blind to check the arrow for blood, hoping there's none, but there is. His heart sinks even lower knowing that it is responsible. There is very little blood, barely visible on the shaft. The blood was only on one side of the shaft and only on two of its four white feathers.

Why couldn't it have been a clean miss? He walks back to the blind, climbs down to get the radio, and climbs back outside. He holds the radio while silently staring at it for an answer, and thinking,

That kudu's all right. In any case we'll never find it. It's just a flesh wound. The arrow grazed the top of his back. He looks at the arrow and the radio, trying to decide what to do. He could wash the arrow off in the water and no one would ever know what had happened, the wounding of the kudu would only be known by Gordon's conscience, his heart, his mind, and God.

He thinks about his rant on the airplane with the compadres and he thinks about right and wrong. He thinks about what the kudu told him, takes a breath, and turns on the radio to call Lucas.

Lucas arrives with his lead tracker, Daniel, two Jack Russell terriers, and his .375 caliber, double rifle. Gordon doesn't like the idea of shooting the kudu with the rifle but he knows he lost his options when he wounded the bull. Even seeing the kudu again would be a miracle. Gordon and Lucas walk behind the tall, thin tracker as he finds and follows the spoor.

Daniel finds only single spots of blood, very few, and very far between. Gordon knows the situation is not good as Lucas tells him the plan for the dogs.

"We'll release the dogs on the kudu's trail. When they sound we'll run as fast as we can to them. You have to run hard and fast, Gordon, if you want to see this kudu again. The kudu will either stay and fight the dogs, or he will run. If he fights we may get another arrow or a bullet in him. If he runs, he probably won't stop."

The dogs sound, the three men run. Gordon is taken by Lucas' acceleration and he runs hard, desperately trying to get ahead of him. Lucas, the overweight, ex-rugby player gets meters ahead of Gordon in the first few strides, knowing too the hopelessness of the situation.

The kudu chose the flight option long before the dogs, Daniel, and Lucas arrived. Gordon catches up just in time to see the dust from the little dogs settle to the earth, far enough to know that the kudu won't be recovered this day or any other.

They track for hours into the heat of the day. There is no more blood and the spoor is only a guess, at best, now. Even the dogs circle back exhausted and dejected. Lucas makes an honest assessment of the situation and tells Gordon matter-of-factly what he knew when the arrow left the string.

"Gordon, you know as well as I do we aren't going to find this kudu."

"I knew that when the string slipped from my fingers."

"You could go back to camp or I could bring you to the blind for the rest of the day."

"Bring me to the blind, Lucas, I'm not ready to face this. I don't think I can see people just yet."

Lucas very diplomatically assures Gordon that this is the very ugly side of hunting that nobody wants to see or talk about but it does happen and sooner or later it happens to most hunters. Gordon knows this, of course, and appreciates Lucas' efforts, but the mistake and the wound from it are still fresh. He spends a long rest of the day in the blind alone seeing nothing and feeling numb.

Lucas picks up Gordon that evening, bringing along a few other hunters in camp. Gordon isn't prepared to see anyone yet, but they all know about the kudu and are there for his support. It softens some of his pain and embarrassment.

At camp Lise is waiting and when Gordon steps out of the truck. She hugs him in front of everyone and says, "I'm sorry, Mr. Bradford, don't worry, we'll get him before the week is over."

"Thank you, Lise, I hope you're right. Could you do me a favor though?"

"Anything, Mr. Bradford."

"Could you just call me Gordon?"

Her voice becomes softer and more personal. "Pleasure, Gordon," is all she says and he feels better. So does she.

At the lodge that evening Lucas tells all the hunters that he's seen animals, hit and not recovered, return to the same water hole or show up at other water holes. The chances of seeing the kudu again are slight, but Gordon has to try. He gives a description of the kudu and where it was hit to all the hunters in camp. He asks that if anyone sees him and can verify the wound, to shoot him.

When the evening ends Gordon walks to his tent alone. He notices Lise's silhouette through the window of the lodge's kitchen. He remembers the kindness in her voice. He wishes he could talk to her, but he knows he can't. The sky has turned to lead, heavy, cold, and gray. The clouds he'd been watching all day break into rain that wasn't due for six more weeks. Rain will surely ruin the hunting. He doesn't care though. When he gets inside his tent, he lies on his cot and listens to the sound of the rain, believing he can feel the relief that it brings to every living thing in the bushveld. He feels bad and good at the same time. He imagines the kudu standing in the bushveld; head down, eyes closed trying just to tolerate the sting of the rain in the open wound. All Gordon knows to do is to send a message out to the universe and, he hopes, the kudu. *I'm so sorry.*

Monkey Mind

*G*ordon hunts the water hole a few more days throughout the week at Lucas' direction. Lucas rotates other hunters in camp into the blind as well. Gordon tries not to give up but with each day hope runs thinner. Unless he is chosen for a miracle he doubts ever seeing the kudu again. Besides, the kudu had told him what was so, and he believes it.

Gordon does manage to take a large blue wildebeest, one from the same herd he had seen the first day. Day after day, they just keep coming back. Gordon figures that blue wildebeest must have been created to feed all of Africa, or they are there just to taunt him while he waits for the kudu. He sits in the hide for days enduring monkey mind, unable to clear his head of the kudu. He tries to meditate but the thoughts come and go with no control. Finally, when a large bull chooses the front parking space at the water, Gordon decides to take what is given, to try again.

He calls upon his mind to stop all thoughts until the killing is through. His mind answers by way of a silent head, so silent his heart is afraid to make a sound. He focuses on one of the wildebeest's dark stripes as it touches the top of the foreleg and releases the string. This time everything goes right. His focus sees the arrow go right through the wildebeest and he knows it's dead standing.

The wildebeest makes fifty yards, turns under a small tree, lies down, and dies. It all lasts about ten seconds.

Gordon begins to pray and give thanks for the good experience, his heart somersaulting in his chest.

Slow down, he says to his heart, *it's over now.*

The heart answers, *that is what a heart does best, it feels joy. Hearts fear the fear, hate the heartache, but they feel joy better than anything.*

He thanks his mind for keeping the heart under control during the shot, and his mind reminds him that minds are for performing and hearts are for celebrating. Gordon accepts that and promises to let his mind be the master of his body from then on.

Mostly Alone

He stalks warthogs in the afternoons to get out of the blinds and be in the bushveld on foot. Lucas appreciates the convenience of Gordon's solitude and doesn't mind letting him wander back to camp alone. It helps that Gordon always manages to find his way back through the network of roads and game trails. Gordon keeps his eye on the sun in the morning when Lucas drives him to the hides so that he can navigate his way home.

During his walks Gordon manages to take a few warthogs, and regain his confidence by shooting termite mounds as well. He experiences some of Africa that he never would have had he stayed inside the hides.

The times he gets back to camp early he spends with Lise, getting to know her, and taking an interest in her life and daily routine in the bush.

$\mathcal{L}ise$

$\mathcal{H}$er day begins before the sun shows itself. Her help makes coffee for some, tea for others, and she prepares the juices, all freshly squeezed, and has them delivered to the boma. She supervises the camp staff in the breakfast cooking and service, and the cleanup afterward. At the same time she makes all of the lunches for everybody in camp, packs them in coolers, fills all of the special requests for the ones with the picky eating habits, and delivers them to the appropriate truck of the PH and client who will hunt together that day. She always smiles at the difficult eaters and says "pleasure" when they ask her to do something out of the ordinary. She fills the request with no bitterness or aggravation. Her mind is filled with notes and she rarely writes things down. She remembers with ease the people she has in camp and the things that they need.

Her morning then turns to laundry. This has to be collected and washed in time so that it can be dried, folded, and returned before the hunters get back into camp. While the laundry is being collected, the tents must be cleaned, the beds made, and the towels changed. Sometimes, for her, having a camp full of hunters is like having a house full of children. She's yet to have children but she is hoping to, knowing that it will only add to her chores. She seems to execute her daily chores with the grace and confidence that they will all get done in time and order, and they do.

Lise never shows stress or worry like a woman who lives in the city. In fact, she is very happy in the bush. She is grateful for the rush and for the quiet. Especially when everybody leaves in the morning, and for the hour in the afternoon when she can sit and the time is hers alone to do whatever she wishes to do.

After the tents are cleaned and the clothes are being washed she might sit for a few minutes by herself. Having a late-morning tea and a snack made from something left from breakfast like a biscuit or pap with honey allows her to focus on the next chapter of her day.

She then prepares the evening meal. She begins by cutting all of the meats, trimming silver skin and sinew, and making their marinades. Moving to the salads and sides, she washes the vegetables, preparing them for later. Everything is stored in separate covered containers in the propane refrigerator for finishing near dinnertime.

Her recipes are laid on a small desk in the kitchen, side by side. Lise reads them all to coordinate the timing of the food's completion and service.

The starters are the easiest to prepare, so she does this last. They always consist of biltong, so this is easy, and she cuts cheese and wraps it and stores it. She removes crackers from the pantry to make sure there are enough and they're not stale. She always checks the boxes and then eats one so that she knows her guests won't be disappointed. She usually serves the dry, white, English water crackers with her starters because they're mostly tasteless and add a good crunch to her cheeses and other spreads without changing the flavor of what she serves, and because, for a cracker, they have dignity. She likes dignity as long as it's not overstated or abusive.

She turns her attention to her staff after all of her plans are in order. She has three people to help her run the camp, an old woman she calls GoGo (Zulu for Grandmother) whom she loves very much and trusts with the responsibility of watching the two other men who also work for her. GoGo has been with Lise for so long now that they work together as one except for the disciplining of the men. The old woman always hands it out with a large wooden spoon and a sharp tongue-lashing. A woman of her background, if younger, would be beaten for insubordination to a man. This old woman cares nothing for that now and she knows that these men, if they want to be fed and keep their hides on their bodies, must work for her and must respect her. She knows that Lise loves her as much as she loves Lise and that Lise will always see that she is safe. So she has no fear of any man.

Moses comes to camp from time to time but only at the request of Mr. VanZandt. He stays for a day or two to see that the camp is running smoothly and that Lise has everything she needs. He also reminds the men that there is an omnipresent eye watching them. He reports back to Mr. VanZandt, and is then reassigned and leaves.

The men are generally good workers within sight of Lise or GoGo. They tend to run in a lower gear when left to perform tasks on their own. Lise knows this about the men and simply plans their tasks according to her schedule so it all falls into place. Instead of letting them work a set number of hours, she gives them the tasks she needs completed for the day and makes sure that they work until all of the tasks are complete. She knows that this is the only fair way to use the type of help that slows when they're not being watched. She's done every task in camp herself and knows how long each takes because she counts everything and times every task. Her high, almost autistic, degree of organization allows her to distribute work knowing that she is being fair to them, no matter how long they take to complete it.

She once gave one of the men four tasks, mow the lawn around the camp, rake the grass and leaves and dump them in the wooded area near the old graveyard, collect enough firewood for the evening and next morning, and take all of the kitchen scraps in the truck and dump them in the bush far enough away from camp that the baboons, vervet monkeys, and warthogs don't come to the camp for handouts. She knows through her own experience that it takes her three hours to mow, two to rake and dump the grass and leaves. She would allow two for the fire wood collecting and one for gathering and dumping all of the food scraps. She gave the man the tasks telling him they had to be completed before the end of the day and left him to work. He proudly came to her that evening saying he'd completed all of his tasks twelve hours after he'd started. Lise felt absolutely no pity toward the man for the hours he worked because she knew the work that went into the hours spent working.

She discusses the evening's plans with the old woman — the menu, and the order of service for all of the foods. They set the table and check the outside bar for bottles that need to be replaced and make sure there are drinks and snacks out for any hunter who may come back to camp early. She returns to the little desk in the kitchen and adds to her shopping list of food and other provisions, organizing it by store and organizing the stores so that when she makes her weekly trip she goes to the farthest first and works her way back toward camp. The trip takes the better part of the day and she gets to see the familiar people at the markets where she shops. Sometimes she phones a friend to meet for lunch. When she gets to town she always feels bad about the high fences topped with barbed wire and the sliding gates that the people have to live behind. It wasn't that way when she was young, but now the crime is so bad that she can only go into town during daylight hours and she has to make sure the truck is full of petrol and the tires have air before she leaves. She always has three cans of emergency tire repair in the back seat of the truck and a small nine-millimeter pistol in a pocket on the front of the driver's seat. When she leaves the truck to shop, the pistol fits neatly into the front pocket of her khakis or into the rear zippered pouch of a purse that was bought just for that purpose. Sometimes she stops at the bank to deposit Lucas' paycheck. She and Lucas work as a team and are compensated with only one check, which is written to him. He endorses it before she goes to town, tells her how much to deposit, and how much to bring home. She doesn't like that subordinate part of their relationship, but in the South African bush it is still the way of most couples.

To compensate herself for the indignity, she started a Christmas account years ago. Every time she makes a deposit she skims a few rand of her spending money into the account that has only one name on it, hers. Sometimes it's only thirty or forty rand but if she is feeling particularly brave, or if she and Lucas have had an argument, she may deposit a hundred. Spite, which she knows is wrong, makes people do things they wouldn't normally do. Sometimes, for Lise, it makes her feel as if she is simply protecting herself from the instability of being a professional hunter's wife. As the years pass with Lucas, she begins to feel like nothing is permanent and the endings are never seen until they're right on top of you. So she saves and the savings, in some small way, help to save her.

With the cleaning and dinner preparation complete, Lise gives the old woman instructions for the men to fill the rest of their day, and then instructs her to tell them to be washed and at the kitchen by five o'clock to help serve and clean. Then she tells the woman politely that the laundry should be dry and to please fold and return it to the appropriate tents before the hunters return.

Now is the time of day that she likes the most. It's mid-afternoon and, if all has gone well, she will have time to herself. Sometimes she gets an hour before hunters begin to return to camp, if she's lucky, she'll get two.

Sometimes she'll walk with Mika, her female Staffordshire terrier, and one of Lucas' best tracking dogs. Mika was given early retirement because she was the most tenacious tracker he's ever had and before she was too old or too badly wounded he wanted Mika to produce whelps of the same caliber. Lise and Mika walk the camp roads and stalk the unlucky warthogs, hares, and small antelope that like the grasses at the road's edge. They hunt, just the two girls, on their own, and when the prey is close Lise whispers, "Mika, get 'em". At this, the dog turns the soil and makes a cloud of dust as her strong, short legs pump the earth like pistons and she's gone. She looks like a little train engine barreling down a dirt road at her prey, and at the point when Lise worries that she may actually catch her quarry she takes the first two fingers of both her hands and makes a chevron with them, puts them to her front teeth, and gives one sharp loud whistle. Mika then slows her sprint to a stop and looks back over her shoulder to see Lise kneeling on the ground, drumming on her thighs, and saying, "good girl, come here now, good girl," at which the dog sprints back to Lise and they laugh, and wrestle, and Mika licks Lise until she can't take any more licking. They've hunted like this for years and it makes them both as happy as a girl dog and a woman can possibly be together.

Other days she simply brings a chair to the lawn and sits at the spot where she can see the vastness of the concession of land on which she lives. It's a feeling, overlooking such a large piece of land that gives her peace. She realizes the adventure her life lacks when she stays behind and all of the PHs and their clients leave in the morning. Sitting on the lawn reminds her how lucky she is, though. She thinks of the people in the cities, living in fear. She thinks of her family and her girlfriends who never made it out. They just somehow never had the money or the courage to leave the devil that they were familiar with, and now it's too late. Lise knows that there's a life outside of the concession that she's missing as well and always ponders the give and take. She usually comes to the conclusion that this life she has is the best life that she's ever known. Instead of wanting for more she needs to remember to give thanks for having more than others. She does give thanks, sitting alone in the yard. She thanks God every day. She gives thanks for her husband who works so hard even though the longer they are together she feels less of a priority than his work. She gives thanks for all of the people who've come and gone in their lives who have supported the way they live, especially for the ones that return. She also gives thanks for the small, quiet, moments that she gets just to sit and be thankful. During these times, when Gordon gets back to camp early, he will sit with her and talk quietly with her, and she's thankful in these times for him, too. It's the quiet talks and the understanding that she rarely gets from Lucas any more. They still love each other but their lives are just different now.

Walking Thabazimbi

To accommodate Lucas' wishes, Gordon is driven to a blind every morning. Gordon stays just a few hours, though, and he calls Lucas on the radio to let him know he's leaving. He brings only his bow, quiver, and a bottle of water and begins the long walk toward camp, the radio bouncing on his hip. The bushveld is ideal for stalking. The terrain is full of brush that allows you to zigzag your way undetected toward your quarry. The brush is low enough that you can see long distances across it and tall enough that in a low sneak you're covered on an approach.

The first animals Gordon sees are impalas, a small herd feeding away from him. He moves in slowly from bush to bush and only when their eyes and attention are focused away from him. Impalas never seem to relax. At eighty yards his knees find the soil and he crawls, painfully slowly, to sixty yards. He thinks, *a leather glove on your bow hand would be great, if you'd brought one.* He read Donnell Thomas' book, <u>Double Helix,</u> just before leaving and it explained the value of a leather work-glove to protect your bow hand from all of the bushveld hazards. Every plant and tree in this part of the world has thorns. Gordon's discomfort is a result of not taking the advice of a more experienced hunter. He can hear Don chuckling, "I told you so," as he presses his knuckles into the soil and picks up a stray thorn. He pulls it out with his front teeth and spits it back onto the earth. A slight swirling breeze passes and that's all it takes to alert the impalas. All heads up at once and all turned in Gordon's direction. He freezes behind a small thorny scrub. They don't see him but they know their lunch has just come to an abrupt end. The impala don't bolt like he thought they would, instead they examine the terrain in his direction sharply for the source of the foreign smell. When their eyes find nothing and their bellies overrule their fear they nervously resume picking at the new green foliage the rain has brought them. Gordon gains more yardage and down at ground level he slides beyond cover and rises onto his knees. He draws and anchors, places the broadhead just above mid-chest and over the front leg of the rear impala. He breathes, burning a hole in the impala with his mind, and releases the string. The impala bound away completing their second leap before the arrow harmlessly impacts the sand where the rear ram used to be standing. Gordon sits back on his heels and laughs at the failure. The sound of the string reached the impala long before the arrow had a chance to. The long-bowman just learned his limits, *if I don't get closer, I won't have a chance against impalas.* Lesson learned. He stalks the rest of the way to camp and arrives with three hours of daylight left. He has a quick snack and water and decides to walk up the river next to camp until dark.

The warthogs have been feeding on the river's banks during the evenings now that the rain has made them green. Gordon hopes to intercept one while walking up a service road that's parallel to the river. Nearly every thirty yards he finds a game trail cutting in toward the river. The trails offer quiet walking to the top of the riverbank where he can check for pork. There are so many trails, Gordon ends up catching them back and forth between the road and the river like a sailboat tacking into the wind.

A half-mile or so up the river he sees movement in the tall grass ahead and on the opposite side of the riverbed. The grass whips back and forth at the top and he can hear it cracking and breaking. He has no idea what he's watching so he slides on his hip slowly down the bank to a small bush to figure it out. A few moments go by and a big, beautiful, mature waterbuck steps out from the grass, turns, lowers his head, and walks back in. It takes Gordon's breath away and for a moment he can't believe he's here and, again, he takes a second or two to give thanks.

Thank you, God, for this place I've come to love so much in such a short time. Thank you for all of the moments, little capsules of time like this, that make my life so blessed.

As soon as the waterbuck disappears three warthogs show themselves in the same stand of grass. They randomly figure eight themselves through the whips of tall grass, seemingly unwary and comfortable in their surroundings.

I could actually have a decent chance if I just move when they're in the grass and stop when they're out, Gordon thinks. With all eyes turned away he begins to walk the tree line on his side of the river, keeping the trees at his left to mask his outline. At forty yards he's feeling pretty good about his circumstances. The animals are still feeding and all he has to do is negotiate the mostly dry riverbed to join them.

He begins to navigate across the rocky bottom of the river, carefully stepping lightly so the rocks don't clack together. They sound like grinding teeth as he tries to walk lightly and he's thankful for the noise of the tall dry grass the animals are in. At twenty yards Gordon is completely exposed when the waterbuck steps out head-on and stares him down. He freezes at a crouch and waits for an opportunity that's gone before it happens. As he looks at the ground trying to avoid eye contact he searches his mind for the right time to draw his bow.

Not now, his mind speaks, *if he turns slowly then draw and shoot. If he spins on his heels then just watch him run.*

What are you going to do? The waterbuck thinks, *He won't shoot you head on, he won't shoot you in the rear either. Set your muscles tight, spin, and bolt. It's the only option.*

The waterbuck spins on his rear hooves and crashes back through the grass to higher ground as if he'd heard Gordon's mind. He most likely did. On the bank he slows to a walk and at fifty yards he turns back to look at Gordon as if to thank him for not making a hasty shot, and then disappears into the trees. Gordon quietly says, "You're welcome, thank you for the thrill." Then he thinks, *this is the time when the hunt is as good as the kill. What a beautiful animal that I'd only seen in pictures before this moment.* Another memory he won't soon forget.

Oddly enough, the warthogs are still in the grass and Gordon is just twenty yards away. He continues across the riverbed towards the disturbance in the grass confounded by the unmindful pigs.

The warthogs are feeding up toward the bank with tall grass between them and Gordon. He makes his final stalk to ten feet. The grass is so thick and loud they can't see or hear him. He knows the heavy arrow can blast through the grass, but he can only make out hams and shoulders and they aren't standing still. He comes to full draw, his mind working fast, processing the visual input and slowing time. Gordon finds what he knows is a shoulder in front of him and releases the string. The warthogs bolt out of the grass and up a game trail running hard, tails up, and snouts down. At fifteen yards the lead pig plows his nose into the ground. It wedges hard as the rear legs continue to pump, then stops in the earth and the warthogs momentum causes it to somersault. It lands with a solid thud, dead, flat on his back. Gordon finds his arrow imbedded deep in the riverbank after passing through the chest of the warthog. At close range, the grass and the warthog seem to have little affect on the arrow's path. It isn't the biggest of the three warthogs. In fact, it is the smallest, but it is a quick, clean kill and a fantastic, successful African stalk. It is also Gordon's first warthog dinner, pan-fried by Lise with garlic and black pepper, and accompanied by a glass of South African red wine. Today, life is good.

The next morning Gordon is shooting at the practice butts before breakfast. He walks to the target to pull arrows and notices a pair of Francolin partridges slowly feeding through the brush far beyond the targets. He pulls a shaft from the target, nocks it, and slowly makes for the cover of the bush. He finds a tunnel through the bushes that leads to a small, clear opening about twelve yards away. The Francolins are pecking their way right toward the little stage highlighted by a shaft of light showing through the bramble tunnel.

It's a strange thing when you know what's going to happen before it happens. When all of your thoughts are concentrated to one and when your mind and your eye capture that one thought at the same moment and your body reacts without any other thoughts, *satori*. Millman says *satori* is body mind integration, or dynamic meditation. It's the inner target of Zen archers. Old guys in archery will simply say they can "see the shot." It's all the same.

What Gordon can see is a single small spot on the Francolin's back as he walks into the opening and before he has a thought the arrow is through the bird and he's nailed to the ground instantly dead. He nocks another arrow, puts an eye on the second bird, and quickly releases trying, but not able, to regain the concentration of the first shot. The arrow strikes the bird on the right side and creates an eruption of small downy feathers as it skips off the hard ground and into the brush. He dispatches the flapping, panicking second bird by trapping its head under the bow limb and apologizes to the bird for its panic. Gordon then helps conclude the bird's suffering by snapping its neck sharply between his thumb and forefinger. The unpleasantness over, he lifts the pair by their feet and admires their features, thankful for their quick demise. He walks back to the lodge for a picture, proud of the little quarry, and gives the Francolins to Lise.

"Gordon, for me?"

"Only the finest of fowl for you Lise."

"But don't you want one?"

Both of them see a candle light dinner for two by the river with Francolins and wine in their minds eye and then Gordon catches Lucas' contemptuous glare.

"I thought it would be nice if my two favorite ladies in camp had a nice lunch on me."

At this GoGo gives Gordon an overt hug of approval, absurdly happy that one of the fine little birds is hers, and everyone laughs, even Lucas.

After the obligatory morning in the blind, Gordon creeps out through the improvised door trying to make as little noise as possible and begins the stalk back to camp. He makes stalks on two different warthogs, gets within twenty yards of each, but just can't seal the deal on either one. Warthogs are a great diversion to otherwise poor hunting conditions. They're fun even when you can't get an arrow in them. Usually they spot you just as you draw and they sprint ten yards or so before stopping to look back to figure you out. They give you a quick look and then an indignant snort as their tails go vertical and they exit the area like little dune buggies sporting safety flags. After two failed stalks, Gordon was ready to loose an arrow.

He decides to sit against a termite mound and soak up the sun that's been absent most of the week. He thinks about Lise and their afternoon talks. How some people can grow close quickly, but time and circumstance prevent a relationship that could probably be extraordinary from even getting started. He imagines two people living their whole lives thinking about each other and hoping, *some day*, but because they are afraid of hurting people on the periphery they do nothing. What they often don't realize until it's too late is that the damage they cause will be temporary, and the world will have a net gain of happiness after it's over. When a couple is unhappy and one becomes happy with another, and eventually the other finds happiness. The world gains in happiness. Then Gordon thinks about the sadness that these thoughts may bring to the universe. He debates both sides until his mind becomes tired because his mind knows right from wrong and doesn't care about the feelings of his heart. His heart asks him to stop thinking and hunt again, so he does.

The next warthog appears as he's walking the main path to camp searching the flat expanse of bushveld that is upwind. He catches a dark spot moving toward him about sixty yards away. It looks like a good pig. It is slowly feeding, making its way between the bushes toward the road. Gordon takes to the ground on hands and knees and slowly moves from cover to cover trying to anticipate the warthog's path. They both change directions several times until some stroke of luck puts Gordon head on at twenty yards. At this he thinks the warthog will turn either direction offering a shot or end up in his lap. At eighteen yards the hog walks around a bush feeding to Gordon's left offering a delight-fully exposed ribcage. Gordon settles to his knees, he comes slowly to full draw, finds the arrow in his peripheral vision, finds a spot above the front leg, and relaxes his fingers. The longbow makes a quick whisper bidding the arrow farewell. This time, thanks to his mind, all is going right. The arrow thwacks the pig hard and Gordon watches as he runs left into the bushveld with the fletch-ing leading him as he runs. It seems the shot is forward into the neck area but Gordon can't explain why the fletching is ahead of the pig as he runs out of sight. He walks to the place the pig was standing when the arrow ruined his day, and checks for blood. He finds a little blood but also finds a small glob of mostly clear congealed fluid. He picks up the small orb of unidentifiable gel from the ground for a closer look. He holds it and rolls it between his thumb and finger, he smells it but can't identify it as either be-longing to a plant or animal. He comes close to tasting it when he thinks about where he is and how many things there are in South Africa that can make your life difficult, especially when you don't know what you're doing. He's curious to find the origin of the orb, but has business with the pig to finish.

Gordon walks slowly toward the tree where the Warthog left his sight. He finds very little blood along the way, which is discourag-ing because he saw the arrow deeply embedded in the pig. He's not quite sure where the arrow entered, and self-doubt sets in as his heart comes to the surface.

I don't like this, says the heart.

It was a good hit, just remain calm and give him time to bleed out. This will be okay, his mind breaks in.

But there's no blood, the heart protests.

The shot was just a little high and forward, the blood is staying inside, and this will just take time.

Gordon puts both his heart and mind to the back of his con-science and begins to pray. He clears his thoughts and prays deep-ly. He prays for a quick end to the warthog's suffering, he prays for finding the warthog, and to be inside the mind of the warthog. On his knees, he gets into a deep theta brain wave in his prayer. He gets only one response, *This ain't over,* and he knows it is warthog speak. It is still alive and it's going to put all of its energy into defeating him.

Past the tree he doesn't pick up any blood so he decides it would be best to go back to the point where he arrowed the warthog, and call Lucas. He waits knowing that the time spent is good for recovering the pig. He pictures the warthog depleted of blood, lying on the ground, having its last breath, and taking its last scrape at the earth with his hooves.

The tracking team arrives with two professional hunters, two trackers, and Lise who wanted to ride along partly to get out of camp, and partly to see Gordon. They start at the place the warthog was hit, and after a brief description of the shot and the events after that, they begin to walk to the tree where Gordon lost sight of him. The trackers find more blood than Gordon did and mark each spot using the toe of their boot to draw a line on the ground. They reach the tree and shortly thereafter lose the blood. Everyone fans out and soon Lise picks up saucer-sized stains of fresh blood on the ground, which amuses all of the professionals working the trail. They get back on track and soon find sizable blood every forty yards or so.

One of the trackers finds the back half of the arrow soaked in blood and dirt wedged into the nock. The dirt jammed into the nock tells Gordon the arrow broke while the pig stumbled or fell.

The professional hunters keep their eyes ever ahead, watching for a run from the warthog, which eventually happens without anyone seeing but them. They sprint toward the warthog and shoulder their rifles, but take no shots. Gordon is glad they don't get the shots and hopes to himself that this can end without the guns. The excitement wanes and they all resume tracking, still finding large blood. Gordon stops at a blood spot to examine it closer and the stain shows dark, thick, coagulated blood with spatters of foamy pink and bits of soft organ tissue. With all of this warthog matter being left, it's hard to believe the pig's still going, and Gordon begins to wonder about his shot that he thought was good. He begins to think this might not end to his liking, but there is so much blood now it must end well.

His wondering thoughts end at the report of two bolt-action rifles firing as Lucas and the other PH fire at the escaping warthog. He runs to catch them as they charge after the pig that is running for freedom when a well-placed seven-millimeter magnum bullet finds the carotid artery of the warthog and relieves the heart of its remaining blood. The hog's aged body skids to a stop and he is finally, without any further struggle, dead.

They all stand and watch as one of the trackers rolls the warthog onto its stomach and cleans the red clay from the bloody orifices. The broadhead of the broken arrow is protruding from his right ribcage, the shaft still in his lung. Gordon kneels close to find its entry point and finds nothing on the head, neck, shoulder, or ribs of the left side, which was facing him when he shot. He examines the rugged, deeply grained, face and finds a vertical slice through the upper and lower eyelids of the left eye. He opens the four pieces of eyelid and sees a wet hollow void where the eye should be. The origin of the gel found earlier becomes plain. This tough, old hog, in the time it took the arrow to leave the bow and reach him, turned ninety degrees from broadside to face Gordon. The arrow entered his left eye, angled through his skull and neck, passed through the right lung, and exited the rib cage. With all of the destruction delivered by the arrow and the burden of the obliterated eyeball, the warthog took six people on a mile-long trek, leaving pieces of himself all along the way. Gordon is convinced the hog would have died without the aid of the rifle but the professional hunters performed brilliantly. Out of respect for the tough old warthog he is thankful the suffering is over. Lucas assures Gordon that the warthog would have eventually died without the guns but Gordon stops him.

"Luc, you don't have to do this for my benefit. I really appreciate the PH speak and the reassurance but I know what the story is. We most likely would have found him without the guns but it could have gotten ugly. The best thing to do in the situation we were in is to end it quickly and decisively and you did that. Luc, you did the right thing. Look at the destruction from the arrow and he was still going. That's one tough son of a gun."

"You should see them tangled in a pack of dogs," Lucas says. "Sometimes you feel sorry for the dogs."

Gordon sits and admires the warthog; with curiosity he examines the deep cracks in his skin, his enormous warts, and the girth of his broken tusks. He is old, big, handsome, and ugly. Both of his tusks are broken off but Gordon doesn't care. He is a great trophy, a great memory, and once again Gordon is thankful. He looks at the warthog and thinks to the old pig, *you're a fighter, a champion, and you're the toughest thing I've ever put an arrow into.* In his head he hears the voice that earlier told him, *this ain't over.* It says, *I am Africa.*

Of Reptiles And Relationships

*T*he day brings a hot sun during the afternoon walk. Gordon finds signs of a dead animal deep under ground in an ant bear hole. Flies and stink are emerging from the hole, enough to catch his attention from several yards away. At the mouth of the whole hole he finds a warthog mandible. He bends over and picks it up for closer inspection finding small bits of muscle still attached. Gordon slips the jawbone in his pocket, still standing in front of the hole. A new found respect for warthogs leaves him wondering what may have killed this one. He squats to get a better look down the hole and a five-foot monitor lizard runs, unseen and unheard, from behind him, between his feet and into the ground to guard its cache of rotting pig. The lizard's tail slaps the side of Gordon's boot before disappearing into the darkness. After gathering his faculties Gordon backs away from the hole, his bow braced to skewer the reptile should he decide that Gordon is still a threat to his foodstore. It never shows itself and Gordon walks home, relieved at not receiving a bite from the saliva-laden teeth of the monitor and tickled with the stolen jawbone.

Lucas has joined him for a few walks when he had time. Gordon lent him a spare longbow and some arrows to shoot. They have walked the bush like boys just having fun. They have grown to like each other, and have even shot a few more partridges for Lise. Gordon has spent more time talking to Lise when he gets back to camp early. He admires her efficiency and organization. She simply does everything well and does it while smiling.

One afternoon they talked for an hour, sitting on the lawn. He should have been hunting and she could have been working, but it didn't matter to either one. Gordon had already made up his mind that he was coming back, and Lise had made up hers that she wanted him to.

On his last day in the blind a single kudu bull comes in from the bush for water. He examines the bull with binoculars for thirty minutes looking for anything that might resemble an injury. He looks at the bull from all angles several times but never sees any indication of a wound. The bull is so similar to the one he shot but Gordon could not find the wound. The kudu and he share the time peacefully until it decides to walk untroubled into the bushveld and out of Gordon's sight. His first safari in South Africa ended without ever seeing the kudu again, just as it had told him. Sitting in the blind that day Gordon wrote:

Even the smallest wounds in Africa may become infected, cause disease, and death. I thank God, predators, and scavengers, for cleaning up my mistake. This doesn't make the gravity of my mistake any less severe, but I'm assured that other creatures may benefit from my error. Eventually the kudu bull will become weak and sick and the leopards will have their way with him. The caracals and monitor lizards will have their share.

The buzzards will circle down from the sky for the rest. The bones will be stripped clean by rodents and insects and eventually the skeleton will recede into the red clay earth. The great-spiraled horns may be the last to go. In the end the only thing left of the kudu bull will be a memory, my memory, for all future time.

Gordon's last walk through Thabazimbi is an evening stalk up the riverbank. He drops from the cover of the trees to look upriver. He walks slowly by the edge of the water. The rains have begun refilling the river. The soil is soft and quiet and green with new life. Ahead of him Gordon sees a branch embedded in the mud and half submerged in the water. On the branch, barely visible, sits the head of a python, motionless with the exception of the occasional tongue flick. Gordon creeps a few steps closer and gets higher on the bank to take a look at the body. What he sees is a beautiful, S shaped, ready-to-strike, body of twelve feet. He sits and watches the python. He thinks what a patient, perfectly created ambush predator it is. He sits and reflects while watching the python's silent vigil until it becomes uncomfortably dark, then walks home feeling very alone.

Moses Counsels Gordon

The old man can tell that Gordon is genuinely good in the way that he lives, the way that he hunts, and that he gives to people, offers help to them, and he takes little from them but insight and knowledge. Gordon knows that the old man is good because there are parts of the world, like this one, where being good is in and of itself a hard way to live. Being bad could be so easy, and just trying to be good makes you good on a soulful level.

Gordon respects the old man and wishes he could be like him, but Gordon carries lust. Lust for travel and lust for the hunt, not for the ego in them but for the experiences they give. He just can't see enough of the world and its people. He can embrace the highs in life and he can even embrace the lows for their lessons. It's the mundane mediocrity of the middle that makes his soul yearn for one of the others. Gordon's main concern is that he knows his time is running out and his lusts are not. He started bow hunting too late and traveling even later. He also knows these are flaws in his character. To want too much can become destructive. Moses knows about lust too. He's seen decades of hunters come and go, some fulfilling their lusts, some failing, too. He knows lust is a burden he is happier without.

"I am sorry about your kudu, Gordon."

"Thanks, Moses, it's my own fault, something I'll have to find a way to live with."

"Gordon, do not worry."

"I don't like to see things suffer, Moses. I've never had a problem killing anything, I just hate to see something suffer."

"Gordon, that kudu will not suffer long, I assure you that. This is Africa, and as soon as a weakness is exposed that kudu will be killed by something. Then many will benefit from your bad fortune. The only thing you have lost is money, Gordon, and that has the least value in this matter. Prey animals must be preyed upon. If they are not hunted they will simply turn into cattle. The other animals at the water hole are smarter for your bad experience. They need to be hunted to maintain their instinct, to hone their skills of escape, and to train their offspring. Predation keeps their muscles and their minds working properly. The kudu escaped you, but it most likely won't escape other predators. In its death there will be life.

"Everything that is eaten, Gordon, is the dead product of something that was living. Even vegetarians are killers."

"Thank you, Moses, thank you for walking me through that."

"Pleasure, Gordon, pleasure."

The Last Night

*A*fter packing to leave Gordon takes his book and walks to the boma for a drink and some quiet time by the fire. He finds himself a glass, puts three cubes of ice and two fingers of bourbon in it. He sits down alone by the fire, opens his book, and thumbs through it, stopping to read a quote. He reads:

"No experience is ever wasted because every experience contains a lesson. The lessons of experience are always positive, even if the experience is not."

Dan Millman

He has a sense of relief that it was all coming to an end and, also, a sense of great anticipation that he would be back again. He has become close to Lucas and Lise in a short time and they him. Gordon wishes he could get to know Moses better but Mo's fidelity to his duty keeps him away from the clients during most of their free time. Then there's Daniel, who has proved to be indispensable as a tracker, skinner, butcher, truck driver, blind builder, and African hunting advisor. Gordon already misses them all as he sits by the fire, drink in hand, planning his return.

"What are you doing here all alone, Gordy?"

"I don't know, Luc, just thinking."

"Gordon, you have to let that kudu go, you made a mistake, you can't change it. You can't rewrite history, you have to get past it."

"I know, Luc, I came halfway across the world for that kudu."

"That's hunting, Gordy, that's hunting. What do you want from Africa?"

"What do you mean?"

"What do you want from Africa? It's not going to give you its animals. It is not going to give you its diamonds, or its minerals. Gordon, Africa's not free and it's not easy. When you set out to take an animal here, you have to know that it can defeat you, and it will, if you make any mistake at all. Just be glad that kudu wasn't a big old Cape buffalo."

"You know, Luc, I've always dreamt about coming here for a buff hunt, so much so that I can picture it, just like I could the kudu."

"Look, Gordon, come back with us. Come back and take some more plains game, then when you're ready, come back for that dagga boy. We can make this work, Gordy, you can do this."

"You know the worst thing about Africa, Luc?"

"What's that?"

"I haven't left yet and I'm already planning to come back."

"That is Africa, Gordon, that is Africa."

He leaves Gordon to finish his drink and sits at the dinner table to write a note.

Lucas writes a thank-you card to all of his clients, a simple note card once commonly used when the world was a more refined place. It's long forgotten in this world, but to give a formal thank-you to his clients gives him great pleasure. It reminds him of his father who raised him to write with impeccable neatness and of his mother who taught him to appreciate people of all walks of life and not be afraid to show it.

Thank You

GORDON,

THANKS SO MUCH FOR COMING TO HUNT WITH US. SORRY ABOUT THE WEATHER, IT'S BEEN UNUSUAL TO SAY THE LEAST. LISE AND I HAVE BOTH ENJOYED OUR TIME WITH YOU, AS HAVE MOSES AND DANIEL. IT'S NOT OFTEN PEOPLE TAKE A GENUINE INTEREST IN OUR LIVES OUT-SIDE OF US FINDING GAME FOR THEM. YOU'RE A RARE BIRD. THANKS FOR BEING HONEST ABOUT THE KUDU; SOME MAY HAVE ACTED AS IF IT DIDN'T HAPPEN. SORRY I HAD TO CHARGE YOU FOR IT BUT THAT, AS YOU KNOW, IS THE RULE. I LOOK FORWARD TO GETTING THE NEXT ONE WITH YOU AND THEN ON TO THE OLD DAGGA BOY BUFF. TRAVEL SAFE, MY FRIEND.

BEST REGARDS,
LUCAS

The Gift

I n his tent, tired from the bourbon, the safari, and the disappointment of the kudu, Gordon pours some water out of his bottle into a towel and wipes the day's grime off of his face and neck. He packs his bags, leaving his cross-training shoes, a pair of jeans, and a few shirts for Daniel. In the front right pocket of the jeans, he places a one hundred dollar bill, and then folds all of the clothes neatly. He tears a sheet of paper from the pocket-sized notebook he carries when he travels and writes:

Daniel,

Thanks so much for the animal education you gave me, and all of the hard work you did on my behalf. Sorry about the kudu, my fault on that. Check the pock-

ets before you let Mama GoGo wash this stuff. See you next year, hopefully.

ALL MY BEST,
GORDON

He places the note on top of the pile of clothes and puts his multi-tool in a nylon sheath on top of the note to hold it in place. He starts to pack his archery equipment and, since he's lightening his load home, decides to leave his spare bow, a few extra strings, and half a dozen arrows for Lucas. He stands it all in the corner of the tent and writes a short note.

Lucas,

You're a good, honest, man. Thanks for all of your help, in and out of the field. You and Lise are the best I could have hoped for. Hopefully it won't be too long before we see each other again.

ALL MY BEST,
GORDON

Goodbye

In the morning the staff is dressed and ready for their clients. The clients eat, hand out tips, and gather their luggage to load into the waiting trucks. Gordon sits alone and stares into the dying coals from last night's fire. He tries as best as he can to absorb the time into his mind, the kudu, the walks, but mostly he tries to reconcile his feelings about Lucas and Lise. He really likes Lucas and respects his work and feels guilty about the feelings he has for Lise. He thinks about Mo, Daniel, and GoGo and he feels lucky to have met them. Lucas watches from the dining table while the other trucks pull out. They are the last to leave but the moment Gordon is having is the moment Gordon needs to have, so Lucas waits, watching Gordon watch the coals fade from red to grey.

A whistle breaks the silence,

"Gordy, it's time."

"Okay, Luc."

"Come say goodbye."

"I'm not so good at that."

"I know, Gordon."

He hugs them all in a single file line ending with Lise. Lucas starts the truck, not wanting to see the emotions, especially those of his wife. When Gordon gets to Lise they try not to let their eyes meet but they do, they try not to hug for too long but they do, neither wanting to be the first to let go.

"Goodbye Lise," he says softly. Her voice trembles as she whispers, "Goodbye, Gordy, please come back."

"I will Lise, somehow, I will."

She looks at the ground to hide her emotions and he turns and climbs into the truck.

"Leaving is usually the hardest part, Gordon. After all we go through — after all of the shooting, the killing, and the work — just saying goodbye is, sometimes, the hardest thing we do."

"Yep," is all Gordon can say as he stares out the window and watches the boma fade from view.

Return to Africa

*T*he planning started as soon as Gordon arrived home. A short trip is all he could afford. Fly in on a weekend, hunt Monday through Friday, fly home the following weekend. A small taste of South Africa is better than a prolonged hunger for it. Emails, plane reservations, and a wire transfer to VanZandt's account and Gordon finds himself back only eight months after he had left. This time Lucas brings him to VanZandt's new concession, Zingela.

Waking early, Gordon slips quietly into a fleece jacket and unzips the tent flap to walk outside. Moses had the coffee ready before anyone else in camp was awake. "God bless that man," Gordon says after his first sip.

Sitting alone, sipping coffee, he watches the sun get the better of a coal-black night. With first light he can see just how big the concession is. Gordon has a view of thousands of acres of his temporary home. The feeling, sitting alone, watching a day begin, and wondering where he fits in this immense puzzle, is hard to describe other than to say it's an intense feeling of belonging and also insignificance. Other than the truck paths, the landscape and daily routine have been largely unchanged through history and Gordon doubts his impact here will be noticed.

Lucas has changed though; he's heavier than the first trip. He's a rugged, solid framed man with the build of a 1970 International Scout. He gives the impression that he can go over, under, or right through anything he wants to. He shows of a man who's dislodged the jaws of a few others in the past but now realizes that kind of activity only allows the local law enforcement to inhibit the hunting for the next day or two, and that's certainly no longer worth the satisfaction of the act. He looks older than Gordon remembers, but the rugger in him still shows. He's a force few would care to challenge. He seems to be more at the edge of ugly behavior too. Gordon wonders about the change in his friend but hasn't found the time alone with him to ask why. What Gordon does know is the life of a professional hunter is a life with many challenges.

A Single Day

It is early morning in late May. Gordon is sharing a blind with Luc and Daniel, asking both men to come along for the companionship and mainly because he missed hunting with them. Waiting for the sun to wash the chill from his neck and shoulders, he can't believe how fortunate he is, how blessed to have this day, and to be in this new place with old friends. It hasn't rained here since February as far as anyone can remember but there is a small stand of red clay-tainted water, a clear sky promising heat that will bring the drinkers, and the hope that every morning brings to a bowhunter in the bushveld. The three men sit motionless, quietly sharing the time in the confines of the blind. As sleep fades they all pick a shooting hole and mind the water.

Their first visitor is a jackal. They share the time with him as he steals a quick drink and leaves. Gordon feels a common predatory kinship with the jackal and intends him no harm as they share the moment. All he and the jackal need is a little water, the luxury of some warm sunlight on a cold morning, and a fair chance at finding game within range. Gordon silently wishes the jackal luck as its day, ultimately, is more important than his own.

Good luck, little man, I hope you find what you're looking for.

As the heat of the sun begins to warm the earth, Gordon whispers, "It feels good to have the sun here with us."

"You'll wish it is somewhere else this afternoon when you've sweated through your britches." Lucas offers, protesting the heat. Then Daniel quietly speaks, mostly to himself, but loud enough to share his thoughts.

"The sun we bless in the morning for its warmth and comfort we curse in the afternoon as it's robbing the water from our bellies, but it is the same sun doing the same thing."

The three men meditate on Daniel's thoughts, understanding that the sun is not the problem. Then movement outside the hide shifts their thinking within.

A lone gemsbok walks to the edge of the water at the left of the blind. Gordon rises slowly to shoot, and then has one of those moments when everything happens in slow motion, his mind taking control before any other interference can happen.

In the blind Lucas sits reading, keeping one eye on Gordon, the other on his book. He knows Daniel is watching the gemsbok for the impact of the arrow.

The gemsbok is at an angle to Gordon's left through the shooting hole, quartering toward the men. There's no shot, but the gemsbok doesn't stop at the water's edge. It walks slowly into the middle of the water hole squaring up broadside with the hide. Without a word from his mates Gordon lets the string slip from his fingers. In the silence of the blind there is the sound of the string letting the others know it is done. Gordon keeps his head down, his eyes on the gemsbok's ribcage, his mind engaged, and watches as the white feathers spin through the animal and land red in the water behind. The blood immediately flows and in that second before the gemsbok realizes something is wrong a thick, foamy stripe cascades down its side, to its sternum, and into the water below. The gemsbok bolts through the waterhole and out of sight as the three men jump to have the last look. They all know it won't get far, and as they sit again, Daniel softly says, "Brilliant," and that is all. Gordon knows they have to wait, so he goes to deep brain prayer and looks for a union with the gemsbok.

My mind knows I'm dead but my legs are still running.

Stop and rest, lie down and die peacefully.

That is the way of the some animals, not the gemsbok. Gemsbok run until they no longer have blood or air.

Then run, run hard and be done the way you chose.

There is no response so Gordon knows the gemsbok has expired. He smiles and opens his eyes.

"What's up, Gordy?" Lucas says after noticing the grin.

"It's done, let's go get him."

"We should wait a little more."

"You're the professional, but it's done."

"How do you know?"

"Luc, you wouldn't believe me if I told you. I just know it's done."

That arrow and its slowly turning white feathers disappearing through the gemsbok's chest and reappearing red on the other side is something Gordon already knows he'll never forget.

Lucas smiles and says simply, "Let's wait."

They sit and wait for the hemorrhage to be effective, and Gordon relives what is, for him, a breathtaking moment. He prays again until his brain waves reach a theta rhythm and it is there that he connects with the gemsbok.

I have left my body behind for you. You won't have trouble finding it. You shot well. I never heard the arrow, I never heard the bow, and I never saw you. A sting in my ribcage and the rush of adrenaline told me I was dead. It was fast and I thank you for that. You and I are forever changed but the bushveld, as a whole, remains the same.

Daniel gets up first and takes a sip of water. They leave the blind and find the red-stained arrow still floating. Gordon takes several pictures because it seems to make its own statement alone in the water. The flies have already found the blood. He whips it through the air to dry the feathers and puts it back into his quiver. The three men follow a liberal spattering of blood, Lucas lagging behind to let Daniel do his work and to let Gordon think that he's doing something to contribute to finding the gemsbok. After a hundred yards through the dusty bushveld Gordon catches sight of what the other two have already found, a mound of gemsbok lying motionless and most surely dead.

"How's that make you feel, Gordy?"

"Not too bad, Luc. Not too bad at all."

Gordon's rarely at a loss for words but at this moment finds it hard to find them. To himself, he thanks the gemsbok.

They take pictures and give handshakes and the truck is called by radio to cart the gemsbok to the salt shed. Gordon walks another hundred meters away from the blind to take a leak and Lucas decides to join him.

"Gordy the Geordie boy, the English longbowman by way of America," he teases Gordon.

"Yep, Luc, it's in my blood, just like being cheap is for a Dutchman," Gordon gives back.

"What do you want to do with the rest of your day, go back to camp and relax, or keep hunting?"

"Lise doesn't need us hanging around camp this early, we'd just be in the way. Let's go back to the blind and see what happens."

They cover the urine-soaked earth with enough dirt to make it dry again and then turn and walk back to the blind. An hour passes and the plains game begin to come and go again as they watch, pointing and nodding to each other but not speaking a word. There's an unspoken, innate sign language in a hunting blind. All hunters speak it to some degree. It helps to pass the time while they wait for the next shot. Hand gestures, nods, winks, and directional stares keep each of them informed as to what the other sees. It's amazing how a man can talk to a woman for an hour and have no idea of the thought she's trying to convey, but three men can sit in a hide and have comprehensive conversations about the world outside without uttering a single word.

An impala walks in from the same side as the gemsbok. Gordon looks at Daniel who gives him a slow and deliberate thumbs up accompanied by two vertical index fingers indicating horns they need to take, so he slides slowly up the back wall of the blind. The impala stands at the far edge of the water alone, offering his ribs, and again Gordon looses an arrow.

At the sound of the string slicing the air the hypersensitive impala pushes forward from of its rear hooves. Front legs off the ground and rear legs soon to follow, the antelope is intersected by the arrow.

"Dang it," Gordon cries out as he sees the arrow bury to the feathers at the front edge of the rear leg. Gordon and Daniel almost jump out of the shooting holes to follow the flight of the impala until he's beyond their vision. Lucas, strangely un-fazed, barely looks over his reading glasses and says quietly, "Well...that just proves you're human." His calmness at the panic of the other two brings reassurance to the inside of the hide. They wait as before, but this time Gordon plays the shot over and over again in his head searching for the answer to what went wrong. Lucas' calmness at the arrow's impact brings Gordon to a question.

"Luc, how can you be so calm?"

"I know my anatomy well, Gordy, so does Daniel. It'll be all right, just give it time. The best thing you can do for a bad shot is to give it time."

Again he prays for a good outcome but Gordon has monkey mind and can't find a calm place to get deep into his prayer. There's no contact with the impala either. Impalas, especially males during the rut, have only one thought, females. No matter if they're feeding, drinking, fighting, or dying, they are thinking of breeding.

The impala circles back to his herd and the females he has bred, and looks hysterically for a female he hasn't coupled. The blood is leaving his thighs with every heartbeat and the herd sees him racing toward them and, as impalas do, they panic and run away. He pumps his legs hard to catch them but the blood he's leaving on the ground is making him weak. He loses sight of his herd and blinks his eyes to clear them, but when he does he stumbles and falls to the earth. His chest hits hard and the momentum of his rear legs spin him around, and for the first time he sees the blood leaving his body. Still looking for his females his eyes dim and his head falls to the ground. The last sense to leave him is his hearing, but not until after he hears the repetitive barking of another impala ram taking control of his herd.

Lucas accentuates his point by reaching into his lunch bag and pulling out a sandwich, a drink, and a small baggie of biltong. He takes a bite then shoves a piece of biltong in with it and passes the baggie to Daniel. As Daniel takes the baggie he catches Lucas' eye and they smile knowing that it's killing Gordon to wait this time. They eat slowly and even tidy up the blind as Gordon looks out of the shooting hole, wondering about the fate of his impala. Finally, after all of the gear is in a neat stack by the door and Lucas feels like Gordon has suffered enough, he cracks the door open, peeks out to see if there's any game behind them, and says,

"Let's go get your impala."

"Finally."

This time Lucas takes the lead with Gordon happy to follow, just hoping to see a blood trail. After sixty meters and profuse amounts of blood, Gordon sees that the end of the impala is imminent. After another hundred meters the two just about trip over the impala before seeing it. Daniel, standing about thirty meters behind says, "I wondered when you were going to see him."

Lucas retorts, "I know, Daniel, you're the best tracker in camp, but I did find him."

"Yes, boss, you did find him. Sometimes that blind warthog can find the lawn at camp, too."

Gordon immediately bursts into laughter, giddy from finding the impala and from seeing Daniel make fun of Lucas' tracking abilities. Then Gordon begins a short but very serious speech:

"You know, fellas, the degree of difficulty for the femoral artery shot is very high. A longbow hunter needs nerves of steel, a steady hand, and a keen eye to even attempt such a shot."

The speech is interrupted by howls of laughter. Gordon turns to look at the pair of them mocking him like baboons, then he sees something new. Lucas and Daniel, holding onto one another for support, laughing themselves into fits of hysteria at his expense. What Gordon realizes is that at this camp, between these two men, there is no color. There is a profound, exceptional, reality for Gordon, and yet another moment he will never forget.

"What's so funny?"

"Mr. Gordon."

"Yes, Daniel."

"The impala jumped at the sound of the string."

After taking photos and loading the impala in the truck, there is still time to spend a few more hours in the blind before dark. It's sometimes unbelievable how long a day can be in South Africa. The rest of this day is spent watching animals but no more are taken except by camera. Mindful of their success, they call the day done a little early, and radio for their ride home.

At camp, Lucas proposes a walk to the salt shed to check out the trophies and Gordon's all in. "Bring your bow, Luc, the hares are coming out to feed on the roadside grasses, one more shot before the day ends may be in order."

The hares don't seem to mind the walkers too much, so Gordon and Lucas make their way to the salt shed pretending they're not interested in the hares either.

"Luc, take that one there."

"That's twenty meters, Gordy!"

"You can do it, Luc, just pick a spot."

"Shoot, Gordon, I'm lucky to see the bugger, pick what spot?"

"Look how the color changes at his shoulder, look for a crease in a muscle, or a shadow, pick one, pick a spot."

Lucas draws and then lets fly a rubber blunt. The arrow misses close, and gets caught in a tangle of grass and thornbush. The hare only skips a few feet and hunkers down. A small cloud of red clay talc holds in the air while Gordon delivers the second arrow. Quick off the string, Gordon's arrow strikes the hare squarely between the shoulders and drives through to the earth below. He ends the day "king of rabbits."

When they get back to camp they find Moses starting a fire and Lise setting out starters. She has Gordon's favorite Pinotage already uncorked. Daniel, it seems, told everyone of Gordon's success and the whole staff wants to celebrate by giving the day a perfect ending. Gordon hands the hare to Daniel and Daniel says,

"Would you like me to skin it for you?"

"No, Daniel, I'd like you to keep it for your own, I'd like *you* to enjoy a rabbit dinner tonight. You deserve it."

"Thank you, Gordon, a hare is a very special creature, sent by God to feed the world, maybe some day it will save us all. I will enjoy it very much."

Making Daniel happy makes Gordon even more pleased than when he made the shot.

There is a satisfaction to the day's end, a quiet kind of contentment that's hard to match outside of a hunting camp. Gordon can't think of a better way to end the day or better people to enjoy the ending it with. He's taken three animals in one day with a longbow he made himself; the shots were all effective with no dogs required. The camp is clean, and dry, and the fire is subduing the evening's chill. Gordon and Lucas are sharing the fire and having sundowners, and at this moment Gordon is pleased completely. Lucas leaves Gordon at the fire to fill out the paperwork for the gemsbok and the impala. As Gordon sits alone he pulls out his notebook and writes,

A day like this is why we hunt for years on end, a single day that will last forever.

At dinner one of the other PHs in camp mentions seeing baboons that day. Gordon asks Lucas, "What do I do if I see baboons while I'm in a hide? Do I shoot one? Or do I just leave them alone? No one eats baboons, do they?"

Lucas unloads his feelings about baboons to all of the guests at the table.

"Other than being an interesting primate to observe, I cannot conjure any warm feelings towards baboons. They are a constant source of trouble in all of our bush camps. They can literally ruin a thatched roof in a matter of days. This also gives them access to the inside of the structure and they will then consume or tear apart anything inside, chairs, mattresses, dishes, and obviously all foodstock. Since most of our camps are remote, restocking involves several long truck, boat, and/or airplane trips to ready the camp for the season. If baboons take over a camp, it almost takes all of our season's profits from us, not to mention the hassle for arriving clients. To stop this from happening, we must keep year-round staff in each camp.

"One of the real sad things with baboons is that they love to tempt our tracking dogs. Once a dog takes up the challenge, it is pretty much a death sentence. It begins with one male baboon taunting the dog and then once the dog takes pursuit, the entire pack of baboons simply tear the dog into pieces.

"Most outfitters place a very low price on baboons. Some even offer them for nothing in hopes that the hunters will help eliminate the vermin. Frankly, they make very good game animals because they are so sharp eyed that they seldom miss a lurking hunter. For bow hunters using hides, they can become a real problem. If a baboon sees, or suspects you in a hide they'll climb to a nearby tree and begin their warning barks. The barking could go on for hours and no game will approach. In rare cases they attack hunters, and if they do they'll take your manhood first before they go for your throat. Not a pretty picture.

"On a moral note, these baboons can be simply gross! The alpha male will couple with both males and females and kill young males fathered by other competing males. Leopards go out of their way to kill baboons, but not necessarily to eat, they just seem to want to kill them all!"

"Well, that lends perspective," Gordon says, not knowing what else to do with all of the baboon information.

"If you see baboons" Lucas says, "your hunting is done". *Okay,* Gordon thinks, *that's a simple enough answer.* Lise sits down at the table between Gordon and Lucas to join the discussion. Gordon lifts the wine bottle to offer her a glass,

"May I please offer you a glass?"

"Thank you."

He finds no extra glass on the table so he fills his own glass and slides it by the base to her. She swirls the wine in the glass, takes it into her mouth, and holds it smiling at the fruity flavors and the earthy finish as she swallows. She takes a piece of meat from Lucas' plate to keep him engaged in the triumvirate, and sips again. Liking her rare moment at the table, she says, "Baboons are disgusting. What they're not killing they're humping and what they can't kill or hump they just destroy."

Gordon presses for more, eagerly awaiting stories of great bands of baboons attacking bow hunters who barely escape with their lives against impossible odds; or how some previous client had shot nine baboons with four arrows, then charged the remaining members with only a multi-tool, and a full urine bottle to dispatch several more before the survivors realize they have no chance against the crazed archer and run to save themselves from extinction.

Lucas says only two more things about baboons, "If they come to your waterhole, the only way to get rid of them is to shoot one". He finishes by saying, "If you shoot one, call me." Lise slides the empty glass back to Gordon, gets up from the table, and as she leaves, says, "I wouldn't want to be out there with a bunch of baboons roaming the property."

Morning Visitors

$\mathcal{A}$s they drive to the unfamiliar hide Gordon checks for landmarks and watches the roads intending to walk home alone. He pulls the compass from his pack and at every turn he gives it a check.

"Better let me come pick you up, Gordy, this one's a little far out," Lucas warns.

"I'm keeping track so if you leave me out here I can make it back on my own."

"The one thing about being a PH is that as much as we would like to sometimes, we can't leave a client behind. That is, unless he has paid in advance. You still owe, so you're safe until the last day. I wouldn't feel good about you walking about alone with a gang of baboons around, so just radio me when you're ready."

"I put an extra arrow in my quiver, I've got four now."

"Oh, that'll help tremendously!"

"I thought so."

"Just call me, Gordon."

He drops Gordon at the blind and they give each other a radio check. Gordon checks both shooting windows as he hears the diesel noise fade to nothing. Sitting alone he thinks about the previous day and the fun the three men had together, but solitude is better for bowhunters so he chose to take this day alone.

Hours go by and not a single animal comes to the water. The sun is high and strong, and the heat of the day brings nothing. *This is unusual*, he thinks, *not a sound, no animals, not even birds singing. It's like the whole bushveld is empty.*

After another hour he begins packing his backpack to leave when a small brown figure walks slowly, silently by the left window. When it gets in front, Gordon sees what it is, a young baboon.

First one, then three or four more, and within a few short minutes his quiet day is full of baboons. They seem to be in small family groups within their baboon community. A large male and female are first at the water with two young ones in tow. Another male approaches them slowly, and cautiously. He gets ten feet from the first family when one of the young ones turns and charges him. The little baboon runs screaming at the big intruder who bolts away to avoid the wrath of this seemingly harmless little child. The little one's family, obviously, carries a great deal of clout in the baboon community. *What an interesting behavior*, Gordon thinks, and he begins to see another great experience where bad luck is not always what it seems. The little baboon slowly walks back to his mother where it gets a nuzzle of approval. It and its sibling return to climbing a dead tree next to the waterhole, and playing like children. Gordon thinks how close to humans they act. He is really not thrilled about having to shoot one. *Maybe with a little time they'll leave without an arrow intervention*, he thinks. Another baboon comes in from the left, climbs up the side of the blind and looks straight in the shooting hole at him. Gordon's frozen before the baboon gets to the window. He avoids eye contact as he does when detected by any animal. The baboon looks at Gordon. Gordon looks down at the ground but keeps the baboon in his peripheral vision. He thinks about what he would do if it were to climb into the blind. *I could probably push an arrow through him by hand*, but then he thinks, *I have two open holes to defend, four arrows, and a bunch of primates. I could be in deep dung here.* He begins to get nervous at the standoff with the baboon voyeur. Then the baboon slowly backs down from the window and walks toward the water with no apparent alarm. Gordon rewards himself with a breath. His thoughts change to maybe shooting one sooner than later.

Another baboon walks in from the left. A lone female carrying in her right hand a dead baby. The baby looks long dead, thin, and empty inside, its little body limp but still whole. She stops on the periphery of the others and begins to clean and groom her baby with all the care you would expect of a mother caring for a newborn. She moves several times. Each time she stops she cleans the baby, smoothes its hair, and straightens out its little, limp limbs. Her dexterity and soft caresses keep Gordon's attention. She and her baby seem to be outcasts, and stay on the periphery of the group.

Maybe she's afraid another baboon may take the baby from her.

He wonders. *What does she think about her baby? Does she realize it's dead, and just can't let go? At what point will she let go of it and leave it behind? What will her final act of love be? Where will she leave the body, and what will find the little rag doll baby?* His heart wavers between watching the mother and the baby, and finding a relative of theirs to terminate.

The baboon intrusion continues for what seems, to Gordon, a very long time. Another comes to look in the blind, and the rest show no sign of leaving. Gordon feels pretty good about the visits at the window, that none of the visitors have spooked, or over reacted to his trespassing at their water. Their numbers ever growing Gordon decides he must shoot one. He stands to the rear of the blind in the shadows and raises the bow. He decides that the next male that turns his back to him will receive an arrow.

A male walks in and sits in front of the shooting hole with his back squarely to Gordon. He sits still and patient, waiting his turn at the water. At full draw Gordon focuses on a single vertebrae and, for a brief moment, wonders what the reaction is going to be when the arrow reaches its mark. *Lose the thought quickly, focus, and release the string.* His mind speaks up. *Don't think about anything except what you are about to do, focus on the spot, nothing else. See the spot.* His eyes focus again, and he relaxes his fingers to let the string slip away.

The arrow blows through the baboon, and they all erupt. They leap and run in all directions. Most make toward the bush, but some go to the trees. Some of them look back at the blind as they run, careen into one another, falling, recovering themselves, and pushing each other out of their path to run again in a confused uproar of escape. The sounds are incredible. Low, unnerving barks to high screams of distress, and locating calls fill the bushveld. A pair of adult males rolls past engaged in an awesome fight. There are teeth, arms, and legs tangled into one another in a large ball of baboon fury. The ferocity of the fight stirs Gordon's nerves as he tries to figure out why they're tearing into each other. They roll past the blind and out of sight. The baboon he arrowed runs straight away and falls flat on his chest at forty yards, momentum carrying him an extra few feet. The arrow passed just to the right of the spine and straight out the chest, it flew through the baboon seemingly not losing any speed and skidded twenty yards across the hard ground to stop in a shallow tree root. For a moment, Gordon forgets to breathe. What an awesome time, filled to capacity with sight, sound, fear, excitement, and a short over-capacity of adrenaline. *No chance I'll see any game after this chaos*, he thinks. As the noise of the baboons slowly wanes and they disappear from view Gordon thinks about the volume of sights, sounds, and thoughts that can fill your mind in a single moment. It takes minutes to process what had happened in just a few short seconds. Gordon pulls a sandwich and a drink from the floor and rests them on his lap without letting his eyes leave the bush outside. As he eats, he peers out the window, thinking that the rest of the day is most likely ruined here, and he might spend the afternoon walking back to camp.

After eating half of the sandwich, he picks up the radio to call Lucas. He clicks it on, and before he speaks there is movement in the bush. Slowly Gordon ratchets the knob to off again, brings the binoculars to his eyes, and finds his little friends, the baboons, are coming back.

Okay, nobody mentioned what to do when they come back! Working the situation through in his head, he tries to decide before the baboons get too close if they're coming to the water again, or if they're looking for the source of their dead comrade. To summarize the situation Gordon has two open holes to defend, three arrows, and the Rudy Ruana hunting knife he's carried for years and does not intend to lose to a baboon. As they filter out of the bush he guesses there's at least thirty of them.

The water's between the baboons and the blind... is it the water, or me? The baboon's approach is slow and cautious and their eyes are everywhere. There is no noise at all, not even from the baboons. They stop at the water and begin to drink again. Gordon eases back into the seat still thinking of the second window, and the situation with his newfound friends. *It seems as if they might settle in for a long, leisurely stay if I don't figure out how to get them out of here. How stupid. Didn't they see what happened last time they were here?* But that happens sometimes when an arrow passes completely through an animal. The animal often has no idea what's happened. There's no report of a firearm, no percussion, and no shock, only massive hemorrhage with very few clues as to why. Longbows shooting heavy arrows are particularly quiet and cause very little alarm, and an arrow on the ground mostly goes unnoticed.

I could walk out of the blind and try to drive them off, I could wait them out, or I could shoot another. He ponders, he waits, and then he decides to shoot the first big male that offers an opening.

The baboons all work their way back in just as they did earlier, slow, quiet and seemingly in the same order. A large male slowly walks in, circles, and then sits with his left side exposed to Gordon. *Well, offer a shot big boy.* On cue, the baboon stretches his arms up, yawns like a human, exposes his rib cage, and then drops his arms again. *Please do that again.* He knows the fate of the baboon. He can see it about to happen. He raises the bow and points the arrow at the baboon's armpit, which is still blocked by its arm. He holds the bow and waits, letting the arrow see its target. The baboon stretches upward again in a big yawn. Gordon draws, anchors, and releases. The arrow's path is as intended. It buries deep in the baboons chest, entering through the armpit, and stops. *It stopped. The other arrow didn't even slow down. Why did this one stop? It must have hit the arm on the opposite side.* By the portion of the shaft still exposed, Gordon estimates the arrow to be through the chest cavity. The big baboon springs to his feet with his left arm raised, looks at the arrow, reaches around with his right hand, grabs the shaft, and jerks it out hard. *I've had it now. He's bringing my own arrow back to kill me with.* The baboon examines the bloody shaft, and then throws it in the dirt, all the while spinning his feet in a hasty retreat from the torment. He runs into the bush and out of sight. The baboons explode again, and after a second eruption of sound, sight, anger, terror, and the smell and the sight of blood, the baboons fade into the bush. He listens as the sounds of the exiting baboons wane to silence and he is, again, alone. He stares at the arrow on the ground for a long time, reflects on his time with the baboons, and the second dead one. He reminds himself how lucky he is to be here, and even though he didn't want to kill the baboons, it may have been the best for Zingela, and his only way to be away from them. Africa is indescribably beautiful, but it can turn wicked and cruel in one single beat of a heart. He clicks the radio on and quietly steps out of the blind to call Lucas.

"Luc, Luc, can you copy Luc?"

"Yes, Gordy, what can I do for you."

"I had some trouble with baboons."

"Are they still there?"

"No, I'm hoping it's over."

"Was it bad?"

"I've still got all of my parts, and they didn't hump me."

"Good thing, brother."

"I'll tell you the story when you get here, but you may not believe it."

"Give me twenty minutes, friend."

"Copy that, see you then."

Gordon sits in the sun, leaning back against the blind. He pulls little black covered notebook from his pack, and begins to write:

For me, it's the unexpected and sometimes unexplained experiences that enrich my life. I could look at the baboons as sabotaging a day of hunting during a short week, or I could be thankful for the experience, the education, and the excitement they gave to me. For me, I am thankful.

As he closes the little book, he realizes he forgot to pray.

Looking For Kudu

*T*he rest of the hunt is spent looking for kudu. Gordon decides to do whatever Lucas tells him to do to find one. When he is in the blinds, he sees every possible antelope in South Africa come in and leave, but no kudu. Lucas and Gordon drive the bushveld for hours glassing for kudu. They make a few stalks but they can never find the right shot, the right wind, or the right bull. They build improvised hides with brush and limbs in kudu bedding areas, only to have the kudu not return.

Gordon spends one afternoon in a tree blind surrounded by giraffes. They come close enough that he could touch them with his bow tip. He studies the differences between the males and the females. He looks several times deep into their eyes and sees the nervousness with which they live. He watches the front mark at the base of the throat on all of them, imagining a heart the size of a basketball that hides behind it. Lucas had a client that shot a giraffe broadside. It took four days of tracking to recover. He told Gordon early on in their relationship that, if he ever wanted to kill a giraffe, he should be head-on with that big mark at the base of the throat, be close enough to put an arrow in the middle of it, and for God's sake make sure the giraffe is calm when he shoots. All of these things Gordon thinks about, over and over again, until darkness falls and the giraffes move slowly, silently, back to the safety of the bush. The kudu never come. Nearing the end of the hunt Lucas and Gordon both feel like they need to talk about the kudu. They're beginning to face the reality that the kudu may not be seen on this trip at all, but neither man wants to suggest defeat to the other, not even the thought of it.

The day before the trip ends, Lucas and Gordon sit in a small hide together. Two kudus come into the water and walk right into the middle. There is a bull on the close side at ten yards with a cow directly behind him. The two stand parallel and Gordon knows he can put an arrow through both if he wants to. He grips Thabazimbi and stands to the rear of the blind, hoping for a sign, waiting for the right thing to do to come to him.

Ten yards, ten stinking yards and I could take both of them. It's no good though; the bull only has forty-inch horns, forty-two at best. He's young, and you can't shoot him with a cow standing behind him. I know I can get an arrow through him and into her too, I know I can. What a feast we will have and Daniel will be so happy. If the male were here by himself would you take him? Probably not.

The mental debate continues because of the lack of kudus, and his desire from the beginning to take one. He looks at Lucas who's calmly studying Gordon and has been since the kudu came in. Lucas looks Gordon in the eye and whispers,

"I can't tell you if a kudu with forty-inch horns is a trophy for you. If it is, then take it."

Gordon realizes that Lucas, at that moment, will support whatever decision he decides to make. As faithful as a brother, he will let Gordon make the decision, even the wrong decision, and stand behind that decision with him and see it through. At that moment Gordon realizes that Lucas' faith in him is more important than a kudu, and he realizes what he needs to do.

Slowly, quietly, Gordon relieves the pressure from the bow's limbs, sits down beside Lucas, and plucks the arrow from the string. Lucas closes his eyes, leans his head back against the blind, and breathes a heavy sigh. The kudus hear Luc's sigh. They look around but don't find the source of the noise. They raise their heads to smell the air and walk from the waterhole leaving paisley mud swirls in their wake. They are the only kudu Gordon sees within shooting range.

The morning of the last day's hunt, Gordon sits alone in a blind. Vervet monkeys and guinea fowl are his only companions, but he takes a lot of pictures to ease the boredom. He leaves the blind and walks back to camp stalking warthogs when he can, but taking no shots. Closer to camp, he finds Lise walking Mika, and decides that if they'll have him, he'd like to walk with them.

"Gordon, you've had a good trip this time."

"I have, Lise, but I still haven't seen that kudu."

"Maybe it just isn't meant to be, Gordon, maybe you're supposed to keep coming back for some reason."

"I wish I knew why, Lise."

"I don't know, Gordon, but we like having you here."

"I wish I could split my time between the States and here, I'd love to see you more, you and Lucas, I mean."

"I know what you mean, we're *both* fond of you too."

They walk, watching Mika chase grasshoppers, catching a few, and promptly eating them. They talk about America and Africa and the things that they like about both, maybe trying to convince the other. They talk about their own likes and dislikes too, and find it very easy to be open with the other. Getting closer to camp they both realize that maybe they have said too much.

"Listen, Gordon, I feel like I've spoken...."

"I know, Lise, I know, we have a lot in common. Sometimes it's easier to open up to someone you think you don't know well, then they do the same, then the more you do the more you trust them, and they you. It happens before you know it, then you realize how fast you've gotten where you both are, and something clicks on in your head and exposes your fears of having said too much. Don't be afraid, Lise."

At this she panics because she doesn't know what he'll say next. "I love you Lise," or "I have no interest in you Lise." Both would be bad, though she doesn't know which one would be worse. She knows she wants him, and he knows he wants her. But it's more than romance, they're connecting on a profound level, and for the circumstance for which they share time and space and can't have each other, they also know that no one is to blame.

"Lise…I just enjoy your company."

"Gordon, you're so kind."

"That's another thing we have in common, Lise, I feel the same way."

"Gordon, can I tell you something?"

"Sure."

"Gordon, when you forget about this kudu, it will come. You can't order it off a menu, it doesn't work that way."

"That makes sense, does that mean you don't want me to come back?"

"No, not at all, Gordy, I do want you back. I'd like you to come back after a Cape buffalo, or just come back with no plan and see what happens. I'd like to see you forget the kudu and just see what happens when your plans don't go the way you plan."

"Lise, you know I'm a planner, maybe to a fault."

"Gordon, let go. You have to plan everything and Lucas has to control everything and the two of you drive me crazy. Come back Gordon, come back for that Dagga Boy. He's here waiting, and I want to be here when you do it. Then let the kudu come to you."

The dog walks ahead as they walk toward camp together. The backs of their hands occasionally, lightly, brush sending those thrilling but all too short chills into the other, but they walk without another word being spoken. The bushveld goes silent in one of those moments where every living thing stops because something is about to happen, and it does.

Mika's Attack

*A*s Mika finds another grasshopper, and smashes its body between her front teeth, three mongrel dogs erupt from the bush and attack her. She fights and panics at the same time but, surrounded by the other three, cannot escape. Lise screams louder than Gordon has ever heard a human voice and runs toward her dog. Gordon knows all at the same time that the dogs must be those of poachers, poachers who wouldn't hesitate to kill him or Lise, and Mika has no chance against three mongrel bush killers. Dropping his bow, he dives after Lise and they fall to the ground. She claws to get away from him, and she hates him more than she's ever hated before. He holds fast to her, knowing the danger they both are in, willing to shield her from the bullets if they come.

Through the dust of the dogfight and beyond Gordon sees a tall black figure running at them and thinks, "Holy crap, here they come."

Not sure if they've been seen Gordon rolls them both off of the road but then realizes the screams make his efforts ridiculous. The black man is at full speed and reaches to the ground without breaking stride to grab a dead limb. Gordon reaches back for his bow and says to Lise in a voice that conveys the seriousness of their situation, "Poachers, stay down." Just the word and her body tightens and she pulls at the soil trying to become a part of it. Gordon takes up his bow and nocks an arrow. Rising on both knees he draws to the cheek, and sees his attacker over the shaft. His eye finds the chest of the man, but before the string slips from his fingers he recognizes something.

Moses... Jesus, it's Mo. He calls out, "Mo," just to let him know where he and Lise are. He swings the bow to one of the mongrel dogs that backed off partly because it's caught sight of Moses running at it and partly to find Mika's throat and finish her. Frozen in the moment Gordon sees nothing but a swollen tick on the dog's ribs and feels nothing but his fingers relax, calmly knowing what is already done. Amidst all of the noise, Gordon hears the sound of the string as it leaves his cheek and feels strangely guilty for the fate of the mongrel dog. The shaft impacts with the dog's ribcage and drives through the far shoulder dropping it sideways over the useless front leg. It howls with pain and tries to escape from the charging man, but in the attempt to stand, it falls on the front leg again. On the next try the dog chokes on the blood coughed up from its ruptured lungs, pushes itself toward the side of the broken shoulder with legs that can no longer stand, then tries to stand once more by planting its face in the dirt and lifting by its shoulders, using its neck muscles because they are the last to work. It falls onto the earth finding no use in any of its body so it closes it eyes and lets what's about to happen, happen.

Moses reaches the fighting dogs and swings wildly at them. He connects with the side of one that begins slinging blood from its mouth as it violently shakes Mika's neck that is still in its jaws. The other has Mika's back leg rendering her unable to stand. Blood leaves Mika at both ends of the attack and she's becoming weak with struggle and blood loss, but fights knowing that Lise is near and she must protect her.

"Moses!" Lise screams as she sees the dogs turn on him. Three shots ring out rapidly, and the Rover drives in from behind.

Luc has a double, Gordon thinks, *the poachers are letting us have it, trying to put room between us so they can escape.*

Lise jumps up and Gordon grabs her and she holds him because she now realizes they're caught in the crossfire between Lucas and the poachers. He pushes her behind him and shoots two more arrows into the bush in the direction of the poachers' shots. The Rover skids to a stop. The percussion of Lucas' big double hits Gordon in the back of the neck and the sound of the shots from behind his head render him deaf. Lucas and Daniel jump out of the doors with guns reloaded. Lucas runs to Lise, surprised to find her clinging to Gordon's back, Daniel runs to Moses who has beaten one dog to death and has the other running after its marauding masters. As Lucas takes Lise from Gordon he whistles sharply and Daniel turns, Luc throws the double and Daniel catches it at the fore end, turning to run to Moses, gun in each hand. Luc looks Gordon directly in the eye to check his intentions. Gordon stares back and communicates without saying anything that they don't have time for jealousy and runs to Mika knowing that she is Lise's next thought. Torn at the throat and thigh and with several puncture wounds at her spine and neck, Gordon knows it is the end of Mika. Lise screams for Mika and as Luc holds Lise, Gordon holds Mika. He turns to give Luc the news using the language of the blinds. Lucas raises his eyebrows to Gordon to say, "How is it?" Gordon looks back and looks down and shakes his head slowly, but only once, to say, "no good." Lucas closes both eyes and nods once to say, "do it," and Gordon nods back to say, "okay."

Gordon kneels, straddling Mika with his leg on top of her legs and his other leg behind her back to keep Lise from seeing her struggle, and because the struggle would break his own heart too. He gently covers her eyes and says, "It's all right girl, just relax. You fought hard, you protected Lise, and she's okay."

The dog pants shallowly and gives Gordon no resistance. He places his fist under her throat then reaches to the topside with his thumb. The blood warms his hand and soaks into his leather-shooting glove, pooling at the bottom. He strokes her throat gently with his thumb to calm her, to show her kindness, and to locate her windpipe. She closes her eyes and Gordon closes off her airway. Her lungs try to draw air but it can't get past her trachea. After several convulsive attempts her body goes soft and so does Gordon's grip on her throat.

"Sorry, girl."

Gunshots ring from the bush and Gordon hears shouting in an African language he doesn't recognize. The big double sounds twice and then some small semi-auto return fire, *probably an AK*, Gordon thinks. Then the bolt-action seven reports, *one, two, three*, Gordon counts to himself, and then everything goes quiet. He picks up Mika as gently as if she is still alive and carries her back to Luc's truck. Lise, seeing she's dead, unleashes some of her grief on Gordon. "Why didn't you help her? Why'd you hide in the grass? YOU COWARD!"

"I was covering you from the bullets I thought would be coming our way," is all Gordon could say.

"He probably saved your life, Lise. If you'd gone running after those dogs the poachers would have shot at you for sure," Lucas says.

Gordon, irate at the whole mess, at Luc, and at Lise walks past them both and places Mika gently into the back of the truck.

"Godspeed, girl," is all he says. He pulls a clump of hair from her neck and places it deep into his shirt pocket for safekeeping.

He walks back to his bow and finds his last arrow and starts for the bush.

"Gordon, stay here," Luc says.

Gordon, emotions on high, points the end of his bow at Lucas and shouts at them both, "STAY...WITH YOUR WIFE!" Then runs toward the bush alone. He pulls the arrow from the dead dog and wipes the blood off on its coat.

Rest well friend, no hard feelings. Not your fault, not mine, just our circumstance.

In his mind he hears the dog, *neither worse, neither better, just our jobs.*

He runs into the bush to find Moses and Daniel, and hears both Lise and Lucas calling him, but doesn't stop. He passes the third dog, dead from the blows of Moses' club, and keeps running until he catches up to Daniel and Mo. Daniel carries two discarded baskets, some dried meat, and a few impala hides. Curiously, Moses is carrying two kudu horns over his shoulder. The horns are stained from red clay, old, and weathered. As the three men meet, Gordon can't take his eyes off of the horns.

"I guess you didn't catch them?" Gordon asks Moses.

"Rarely do poachers get caught, Gordon."

"At least nobody was hurt," says Daniel.

"Can I see those horns, Mo?"

Gordon takes off his wet shooting glove, takes the horns, and rubs them clean. He lays them on the ground and stares at every inch from the rodent chewed bases to the ivory tips. One, he finds, is chipped. He lays them on the ground, and places them as if they were still worn by their owner.

"A good young bull," Moses says, "not killed by the poachers."

"I know, Mo, it was killed last year."

"I know, Gordon, by an arrow."

"That was my thought."

"How do you two know this?" Daniel asks.

"It's Gordon's kudu, Daniel, we've finally found him."

Gordon looks at them for a long time, remembering the chip, and the ivory tips. He says to everyone, including the kudu, "Let's go home."

Leaving Again

"Gordon," Moses says very seriously, "home is where you are going, now."

"I know, Mo, I leave in the morning."

"You are leaving today, Gordon, as soon as you can pack. We're taking you to the airport and you're getting on the first flight out of South Africa."

"What the heck are you talking about, Mo?"

"Gordon, your arrow hit one of the poachers." He pulls the blood-soaked arrow from his back pocket to show Gordon. The white feathers are wet and flat from being drawn through flesh. "As soon as they reach town they'll tell everyone about being shot by a white man at Zingela. By the time the townspeople get back here they'll want your hide in return. You, Lucas, and Lise need to be gone as well as all of the other hunters in camp."

"Moses, they were shooting at us, they were poaching animals, and they were trespassing."

"It doesn't matter, Gordon, you're a foreigner, a white man in Africa from a foreign country. You can't shoot the native people and keep enjoying your holiday, no matter what the circumstance. The poachers are purveyors of black-market meat, local Robin Hoods. They have support of the townspeople. They *all* will be here soon, machetes in hand, seeking revenge. Any white hunter in camp will be hacked to death."

"Mo, I was defending myself, and Lise. I was doing the only thing I could to help you."

"It doesn't matter now, Gordon, it is done, and we have to go."

The three men run from the bush to Lucas' truck. Moses, talking fast in Afrikaans to Luc, explains the situation.

"Crap, Gordon, what did you do?"

"I defended myself, and your wife. A minute ago you were telling her I saved her life."

"You can't do that here, Gordon."

"You can't defend yourself, Luc?"

"It's different here, you have to let the professionals handle the ugliness."

"We were being shot at!"

"I was handling it."

"The hell you were, you were still in the truck!"

While Lucas and Gordon argue the finer points of nonresident assaults on resident poachers, Moses contacts VanZandt on his sat-phone.

"Mr. Van, we have trouble at Zingela."

"Baboons again?"

"No Mr. Van, one of our hunters shot a poacher with his bow."

"Details later, Mo, what do you need right now?"

"I need all of the hunters and all of the guests out of this camp in an hour. I need the police here before the villagers get here, and I need you here as soon as possible."

"I'm getting too old for this, Mo. All right listen, we've been through deeper dung than this together, and we will get through this. Get on the radio…"

Lucas begins shouting into his radio, "All PHs LISTEN, get your hunters back to camp. EVERYONE back to camp. POACHERS, POACHERS, POACHERS, on the property, get all of the clients to camp."

Mr. VanZandt continues, "And get all of the clients and their gear loaded in the trucks of their PHs. Get them over to the Manzi farm, I'll get old man Manzi on the phone and let him know the situation. Who shot the poacher?"

"Mr. Gordon Bradford."

"The longbow guy!"

"Yes."

"Figures, get him in plain clothes, tell him to leave his gear, take no camo, no hunting stuff, and get his PH to get him to the airport. He'd better have a credit card 'cause he's going to get on the first flight out of South Africa he can get on, I don't care if he has to go through China to get home, just get him out. Who's his PH?"

"Mr. Lucas."

"Have Lucas and Lise to get him to Johannesburg, then stay away. Don't come back until we call them."

"Yes, Van."

"Moses, you and GoGo figure out what you're going to say when the police get there and what you'll say if the villagers get there first. Be strong, Mo, I'll get there as soon as I can. Pray that Mr. Bradford didn't kill him."

"I already have."

At that VanZandt hangs up and calls the Manzi farm to explain his situation and see if they can make room for his people. The Manzis recognize the urgency and send a man to wait at their gate for the clients from VanZandt's farm. Lucas and Lise grab some clothes and all of the cash and valuables they have in case the camp gets raided and change into street clothes. Gordon throws his bow and arrows back into the travel tube. He stuffs all of his hunting gear into it and then crams his camo clothing in it after taking Mika's hair out of his shirt pocket. He throws the bloody shooting glove under his cot, washes quickly, and puts on khakis and his travel shirt with the hidden pockets. He finds his watch, wallet, and passport, then grabs his backpack and duffle and runs to Lucas' truck. He sees Daniel, worried and waiting.

"Daniel, this is going to be all right. We didn't do anything wrong. My bows and all of my gear are in my tent, you can have it all."

"What do you mean?"

"All of it Daniel, the bows the arrows, the quiver, and the clothes. It's all yours now, hunt well Daniel, and Godspeed."

They shake hands.

"Good luck, Mr. Gordon."

"Good luck, Daniel, I'll see you next year and this will be a great story."

"Let us hope so, Mr. Gordon."

"Daniel, you're a smart young man. Think, pray, and you'll find a way. Ask for it, it will come to you."

"I will, Mr. Gordon."

"Daniel, you're as much a man as I am, probably a better one at that, just call me Gordon."

"Good luck, Gordon."

"Good luck, Daniel."

Lucas whistles and says, "Gordy, get in. Daniel, get all of the clients out of here and then get to the bush. You know this place better than anyone, get out there and sleep in the blinds, keep moving, and stay in touch with Moses when you can."

"I will, Lucas."

"Daniel, I'll pray for you."

"Lucas, I'll pray for you too."

"Why?"

"You have to go live in the city."

They both smile at each other and shake hands for an extended time. Lise jumps into the Rover, and Lucas climbs in and they leave their home and their family behind.

The Camp Is Closed

*D*aniel finds Moses and GoGo making plans for the coming assault from the villagers. Another PH in camp walks into the kitchen and asks about the situation. Moses instructs him to get every client in camp loaded and gone. He tells Daniel to help clean out all of the tents like the camp is closed. They both run.

As the clients and their gear are loaded, the explanation the camp has been invaded by poachers is all that's needed to get them to go without protest. Daniel gets the last of the bags loaded and has only Gordon's bow case left. He decides to bring it to his tent. The three other professional hunters in camp get in their trucks and leave, driving out of Zingela and over to the Manzi farm bringing everything of value with them.

A Single Moment in Time

Sitting on his bed with the case across his legs, Daniel begins to pray. He prays deeply, goes far inside himself, and reaches further to God than he ever has. He is scared for the first time in a long time. He opens his mind completely and clears his head of all thought and just tries to listen. An answer comes.

Daniel opens the case filled with Gordon's hunting gear. He slides out a longbow, a handful of arrows, and Gordon's handmade deerskin quiver. He drops the arrows into the quiver and sets it to the side. He pulls out one of Gordon's camouflage shirts, now his. He's never owned one before. He pulls it on over his tee shirt, buttons it from the top down, and buttons the sleeves tight using the second buttons on the cuffs. He removes the new leather, shooting glove, Gordon's spare, from the case and stretches it onto his hand stopping for a moment to smell the tanned elk hide. He ties the quiver onto his back, and walks out of the tent. Daniel stands and bends the bow over his knee as he has seen Gordon do dozens of times. With his right hand he slides the loop of the bowstring up the limb and into the string groove at the top. Easing off of the limb the bow stands braced and ready to shoot. Daniel lays an arrow carefully on the shelf and nocks it onto the string. Wrapping three fingers of his right hand around the string, one above the arrow, two below, he takes the bow skyward in his left hand and pulls the arrow to the corner of his mouth. Without moving anything, holding solid with his bow arm, he releases the string. The string whispers and drives the arrow skyward as Daniel watches, awed by the beauty of the flight, the speed of the limbs, and the sound of the string. The arrow disappears into the bush, never to be seen again, except in Daniel's memory. A single moment in time, it finds a place in his soul where his ancestors reside and speaks to them. Then they speak to him. He turns and walks to the boma.

Along the way, he nocks arrows and shoots at bushes and termite mounds and realizes he can hit pretty close to what he looks at. Something in him lets him feel that the situation will turn out good, so he walks with no rush, and he shoots.

Saving Zingela

$\mathcal{M}$oses and GoGo decide between them they will tell the villagers the camp is closed and there are no hunters, both of which are true. They will say that the poachers are trying to get a mob to loot the camp because they know it is empty and undefended. They will tell the invaders that the only people who will be harmed are other Africans.

VanZandt contacts the police but they seem disinterested in being hurried to a dangerous situation by a frantic old man. They promise to get there as soon as possible. He rushes on toward Zingela without them, and as luck or fate would intervene, gets pulled over for speeding. In his panic to get to Zingela he explains to the police officer what is happening at his camp and the devastation he may find if he doesn't get there soon.

"What would you like me to do about that, Mr. VanZandt?"

"Follow me there and help. You are an officer of the law."

"Yes, and I have my assignment here."

"I know, writing speeding tickets and letting people pay you directly for them."

"What are you implying, Mr. VanZandt?"

"Listen, I've lived here my whole life, I speak six languages, I am an ombudsman for tribal affairs, I am no stranger to African business deals."

"Are we making a deal, Mr. VanZandt?"

"I need your help. I'll pay you a thousand U.S. per car for both of the cars you have here if you can get to my camp in a hurry."

The policeman walks to his fellow officer and explains the situation. The other policeman starts his car and the first returns to VanZandt and says,

"We will turn our lights on, but you lead the way."

"Try to keep up with me," VanZandt replies.

Daniel and the Hare

The long, black, sinewy muscles of his shoulders and triceps strain to hold the bow still while its limbs reach full stress. Daniel looks over the top of the shaft and sees a hare beyond it feeding on grass. He doesn't judge the distance, he doesn't aim in any manner at all, he just stares at the base of the hare's ear, and he thinks of nothing else. The string leaves his fingers and the arrow finds the location, although slightly lower and further back, and it severs the hare's neck. The hare dies without knowing what killed it, but it did see Daniel just as he released the string.

As he picks up the hare and puts the arrow back in his quiver, he looks at his kill with pride, with sorrow, and with peace that there is a plan for everything.

I'm sorry, rabbit, but you were sent here to save.
I know. That's what hares do. We are here to feed the world.
You will do more than feed, rabbit, you will save.
I don't understand, aren't they the same?
Sometimes yes, sometimes no, this time not at all.
I am just a hare, I don't understand you, but use my body well.
I will, rabbit.

I Didn't Lie

The villagers break the gate and walk, drive and ride bicycles, carrying with them sticks, pipes, and machetes.

As the first arrive, Moses meets them at the boma.

"What are you doing at my camp?"

"We are here to kill the white hunter who shot our brother with a bow."

"You are here under false pretenses. There are no hunters here. Camp is closed."

"We were told the story of the white hunter who shot our brother."

"Again, there are no guests in our camp."

"We will burn your camp to the ground to find the white man who shot our brother."

"I am only one man here with one old woman and a few camp helpers. I cannot stop you, but I can tell you there are no whites here, and you will not find what you are looking for."

"Then you should prepare to die, old man."

"I have been prepared to die since the day I could read. I am secure in my heavenly rewards and there is nothing I cannot endure on earth that won't be worth getting them. Leave the old woman; she has no part of this situation. She is just our cook. Take the camp, do what you want with me, but leave GoGo be. I am ready."

"This won't be easy for you, old man."

"It is your burden to bear, not mine. You will live with your actions long after I have gone to my reward."

"WAIT," a young man shouts from across the boma. Daniel walks up to the crowd and steps directly in front of Moses. He is still wearing the back quiver and carrying the bow.

VanZandt arrives with the two police officers in tow, just in time to see the young man take control.

"What are you doing at my camp?" Daniel asks the man in the front of the crowd.

"We are here for the white hunter who shot our brother."

"There are no white hunters in the camp, it is closed. There is, however, a black hunter."

The policemen, seeing the size of the crowd, elect to stay disengaged, content to be onlookers. VanZandt is urged to stay near them and let the current negotiation continue.

"What do you mean, a black hunter?"

"There is just me here, shooting hares."

He pulls the hare from his pocket and holds it in front of the man close enough to make his point. The man slaps it out of his hand and the hare falls to the ground. Daniel gently picks it up, dusts it off, and puts it back into his pocket.

"The man that shot our brother was a white man."

"Did you see him?" Daniel asks.

"No, but I was told. There were other white men shooting at our brothers too."

"Did you see them?" Daniel challenges again.

"No, but I was told."

Daniel continues, "My brothers, let me tell you what I know to be true about the events of today. Earlier this day the lady of the camp" — he looks directly at GoGo, implying it was she but not saying so — "was walking her dog. Earlier this day I was hunting for hares with my bow. Earlier today this old man was at camp close enough to hear the lady scream. The woman's dog was attacked by those of the poachers, it was torn to pieces by the mongrels right in front of her eyes."

GoGo begins to cry for Lise having to watch Mika being torn apart. The crying is not forced. But it is fortuitous.

The crowd begins to see that there may be merit to what Daniel has to say; they begin to see more perspective of the poaching trade.

"The woman screamed and the old man and I both came to help. The poachers, who had cut our fences and entered our camp illegally, began to fire their weapons at us, me, the old man, and a woman with a dog. The old man fired back at them and yes, my brothers, earlier today I shot an arrow into the bush and I don't know where it landed."

"It landed through the shoulder of our townsman."

"It may have, it may not have. I told you I did not see my arrow land. I only saw it fly into the bush and out of my sight. After *your* poachers ran, we found baskets of dried meat, impala skins, and two kudu horns they were stealing from this camp. If your townsman was shot here, it was because he was trespassing, poaching, and trying to murder an old man, a woman, and me. He committed offenses against the people who keep this camp running, and now you are here to defend his actions because you believe a story that was told to you by him and his thieving brothers.

"We have the police here and they have heard the truth by someone who has actually been here. Everything I have said is true. We have the owner of the concession here. He is the only white man in camp and the police can verify that he came with them. He came because he was concerned for our well-being as soon as we told him we had poachers in camp. If you should still want revenge after what I have told you, then you should take me first."

Then Daniel looks the captain of the vandals in the eye. He pulls an arrow from his quiver, nocks it, and brings the bow to full draw in one fluid motion. Without a blink he says just one last sentence,

"If it is revenge you seek, first dig two graves."

The police grip their rifles tight, VanZandt watches, hardly able to breathe. He always thought he would die in the bush, an elephant maybe, or a buff charge, a jammed rifle that does him in. He never thought he would be hacked to death by a misguided mob looking for misplaced justice. For a time no one at the boma knows what the outcome will be. No one, that is, except Daniel. Daniel knows the battle of good and evil, he's lived it once already in his young life. He succeeded then and he knows now he will succeed also. It was in his prayers, and he has faith in the visions of his prayers. He also has faith that he learned from Moses that if he is murdered today, that will be okay too.

The bow strains to be released because that's what bows want the most, to rocket a shaft forward and split the air. The arrow aches to split bone and flesh and prove its penetrating power. Daniel pulls deep into his shoulders and holds unyielding to the string. The man in front of Daniel breaks his stare into Daniel's eyes and looks at the sharpened steel broadhead at the end of the shaft pointing at the bridge of his nose. His face is strained because he knows there are only earthly rewards for him, and if he dies today he will no longer be able to thieve them. He looks at the hare hanging from Daniel's pocket, dead from the same man with the same bow. He knows there is a decision for him to make before it is made for him and he knows his followers are watching.

Without a word or a sound the captain of the vandals turns and walks away. Amazed at the bravery and the conviction of the young man, the crowd turns and follows.

Daniel holds the bow at full draw, empowered by the burn in his shoulders. When the crowd is fifty meters away and no longer looking back, he slowly lets the string down, pulls the arrow, and drops it high over his back into the quiver.

GoGo grabs Daniel like a grandmother and sobs with happiness, lingering fear, and pride. Moses puts a hand on his shoulder and simply says, "You performed well, Daniel."

Daniel looks to Moses and says, "I didn't lie."

"I know, Daniel, I know. You are my teacher today."

The police, having done nothing to fulfill their obligation, look to VanZandt for their money. He obliges, feeling as if he's on the bad end of a used-car deal.

"At least stay until they're gone."

"Certainly, Mr. VanZandt, is there any food in camp?"

"Certainly, officer, just see Miss GoGo, she can fix you anything you want."

"The camp is fully stocked for guests, Mr. VanZandt?" the policeman enquires.

"We're expecting them soon. We'll have to patch the fence and fix the gate before they arrive."

"Then we will see Miss GoGo and let you attend to your work."

Van doesn't mind the cupboard raid by the officers because it will keep them in camp until he's sure the trouble is gone. He walks to Mo and Daniel.

"You're a brave one, Daniel, I don't know how to repay you."

"I have someone stronger than all of those men on my side, sir, and it is my duty to my home and my family here. This is my place, my animals, and my clients. They are all in my care."

"Son, as long as I breathe you will have a job with me and when Moses wants to retire, you can have his."

"That is very kind of you sir, but I am happy just being a simple hunter."

"Then a hunter you are, and, whenever you have time away from clients, you take that longbow of Mr. Bradford's and you hunt."

"It is my longbow, sir. Mr. Bradford gave it to me along with all of his hunting gear."

"Then you have one more responsibility when you can fit it into your schedule."

"What is that, sir?"

"Providing meat for the camp."

"Sir."

"Yes, Daniel."

"Now I have been repaid."

The best thing that Daniel could ever hear is he can hunt for himself. He loves hunting with the clients, but hunting on his own is something that he's never done before.

VanZandt walks to the kitchen to check that the police officers are getting their fill but not taking too much advantage of Miss

GoGo. Daniel and Moses walk toward the tool shed to get the baling wire, barbed wire, and the tools to repair the front gate and the hole in the fence made by the poachers. Moses puts his arm around Daniel's shoulder and says,

"Daniel, I've seen some of the worst and some of the best that Africa can show a man. My father was murdered when I was a young man, I met a man stuck in the past, hunting like our ancestors did, and then there is you, Daniel."

"Me, Moses?"

"Yes, Daniel, today you are the arrow from my quiver."

"Your arrow?"

"Psalm 127, Daniel. 'Like arrows in the hand of a warrior are the children of one's youth. Blessed is the man who fills his quiver with them. He shall not be put to shame when he speaks with his enemies at the gate.' Today I only needed one arrow, Daniel, you. That was one of the bravest things I've ever seen a man do. Son, I'm very proud of you."

The words bring a torrent of emotions and, although he tries, Daniel cannot hold back the tears. The one sentence he's been waiting for his entire life reduces him from a hero to a child momentarily, then it fills him with pride. That one sentence was worth risking his life.

Gordon's Departure

The Rover pulls into the departure lane at the airport. Lise hasn't said a word during the entire drive. She's overcome with grief for Mika, fear for the camp, and working through in her mind how she feels about Gordon. Lucas internalizes all of the stress and focuses on getting his client out of Africa. Gordon realizes the seriousness of the situation and is nervous for everyone involved except himself.

"Gordon."

"Yes, Luc."

"I didn't have time to write you a thank-you note."

The two men chuckle like schoolboys knowing they're close to getting away with something without getting caught, but they're not quite there yet. Lise stares ahead, wondering why they don't see what she's going through. The Rover stops and Gordon wastes no time getting out, he throws on his backpack and lifts the duffle onto his shoulder. He leans into Lise's window and into her personal space and shakes Lucas' hand.

"We had a good one, friend, I hope I didn't muck things up too bad for you."

"I'll send you the bill."

"Seriously, Luc, let me know what happens, I'm worried about the folks we left behind."

"Me too, Gordy, Me too… Gordon."

"Yes, Luc."

"Thanks for watching over Lise out there…really. That could've gotten very ugly for her."

"Pleasure, friend. Goodbye, Lise."

Since he's in her space already and he figures he's lost it all, he kisses her on the cheek and pulls himself out of the window, the taste of her tears on his lips. He looks at both of his friends as they leave. She says nothing at all. She's in shock from the dog, leaving GoGo, and now a kiss from the man she thinks she hates more than anyone but may also love. *Africa is so beautiful,* she thinks, *until it blows up in your face and there's death, destruction, and panic all around you. Then the blood and horror simply soak into the soil and are gone. It gives you the birds, the flowers, and your beautiful life back and you go on like nothing happened. It fools you into thinking the beauty is going to be forever, but it never is, there's always a sacrifice.*

She has no idea what to feel about Gordon, she knows it shouldn't just end like this but the shock of it all has her frozen. He turns and walks toward the airport. As the Rover pulls off Gordon looks back for Lise. She looks for him too, and their eyes meet, but her tears distract his thoughts.

Askari and the Dagga Boy

A restless herd of Cape buffalo grazes through the South African bushveld under an evening sunset of blended orange and pink. As they pass an isolated baobab tree, a young bull grazes close to the herd's oldest and most dominant bull.

The rest of the herd is anxious with the anticipation of trouble from within. The old herd bull is now being referred to as Dagga Boy, a name given to an old bull who has survived hunters, challenges of other bulls, and lived long enough to be discarded by the herd to which he's given his courage, his faith, and his genetics.

This is how it has always been in the Cape buffalo herd and the old bull knows it is coming. He remembers it happening to others, but now he realizes just how hard it may be. He feels an ache like a stomach full of stones as his herd disconnects from him. There's no more eye contact from them, they've already let him go inside, and this, to him is greater than any blow from the bosses of any bull he's ever battled. The only one with him is a young herd bull, an Askari, a policeman of sorts, sent to keep watch after the old bull until a hunter takes him, the lions have their way with him, or he simply lays himself into a mud wallow and wills himself to stay until he expires. The Askari is to stay with his Dagga Boy and keep him safe, be his eyes and his ears, and keep him alive as long as possible. Negotiations between the Dagga Boy and the Askari begin.

"Dagga Boy, come with me," says the Askari. "We must go, the other bulls are growing angry you're still here."

"I've spent my entire life in this herd," says the old Dagga Boy. "I always hoped that my time to leave would be of my own choosing."

"But, Dagga Boy, you know you'll never leave unless they force you. All of your cows and all of your calves are here. You've helped to build this herd, you've passed your genes, but now we have to go. The bulls want you out of their way so they can fight for the cows."

The Dagga Boy chokes back a mouth full of dry grass that he's pulverized with his almost toothless gums and says, "I can no longer defeat the other bulls, but they still see me as a threat. My old age has taught me much treachery, they know that, and they won't yield until I leave. I can still cause great damage to them, but when they stand together against me, I can't stay. I did the same to the Dagga Boys before me and now it is my time."

The young Askari replies, "Yes, Dagga Boy, we must go before there's trouble."

"No, Askari, I won't run from my own herd, I will not leave them, and I will not hide from them."

"But, Dagga Boy, the other bulls want us gone now."

Solemnly, the Dagga Boy explains, "Askari, they will not come for me. They may be stronger and younger, but they know that I've killed more and I've killed better than they know how. They know that they're the future of the herd, but they also know I won't hesitate to gore one of them a gaping wound if they try for me. They're smart enough to know that it's not a good way for any buff to die. Askari, this is what we are going to do. We are going to stay right here. We are going to stay right here and we are going to graze and we are going to watch our herd as they move on and leave me. I will not leave my herd, Askari. I will watch, though, as they leave me."

The Askari, swollen by his own youthful pride, says, "You know, Dagga Boy, they will *all* leave with the dominant bulls. They won't stay to guard you, except me. I am your Askari, your policeman."

"You're a good young bull, Askari, I've raised you well and you've learned much in your life. Some day, you will be a dominant bull."

"Yes, yes, Dagga Boy, I'll fight the other bulls when I'm able, I'll fight the lions, and I will fight the hunters too. But now I belong here with you."

"Yes, Askari, in your time you'll fight them all. Some you'll be ready for, and some you won't, but every time you do you'll learn," advises the old bull. "Remember, Askari, remember your lessons, the more you remember, the longer you'll live."

Setting Things Straight

*G*ordon and Lucas sit miles away enjoying the same sundown with drinks and starters. They're as content as any two men can be. The only way Gordon could make up for the carnage of the last trip was to come back again, overspend, over tip, and apologize at every opportunity.

"Lucas, you know, I really am sorry for the problems I caused you."

"Me, I didn't have to do anything but take you to the airport a day early. I was fine. VanZandt was fit to be tied, though."

"I've made good with him, Luc, I've got the wire transfer to prove it."

"I'll bet you do."

Lucas stuffs two fried chicken feet in his mouth, follows them with a swallow of lager beer and says, "Gordon, you know we've made several good stalks on buffs but that longbow is an incredibly difficult instrument to work with on an animal like this."

"Lucas," Gordon explains, "if I wanted easy, I'd have taken your rifle four days ago and shot the first bull with solid bosses we stalked and we'd be fishing now. You've put me in front of several small herds and small bachelor groups and I think you're doing a fine job, but you have to understand I need to take the lead when we stalk or we'll never finish this well."

Lucas' beer glugs twice and he swallows and says to Gordon very directly, "My friend, my first duty on a buff hunt is to keep you alive, my second is to get you your buff. If I put you out front with that stickbow, neither may happen."

"You're just used to rifle hunters. No offense, but I can't manage a stalk to twenty yards, get in a broadside position, draw and release an arrow while I'm sniffing your crack! Traditional archery is a very solitary undertaking, Lucas, you simply can't walk up to a herd with your client, three trackers, and a .500 nitro, unfold the shooting sticks and tell him to shoot above the foreleg from a hundred yards."

Lucas is not sure whether to laugh or be offended so he says nothing for quite some time, gathering his thoughts before his mouth reacts. Gordon wonders to himself what the big deal is. The truth is simply the truth; no offense should be taken by simply speaking the truth.

Lucas speaks softly, "Gordon, I've had a run of bad luck lately. To be honest, I've had a bad year. I've had a lot of client mistakes that have landed in my lap, and I've made a few of my own. I feel older than I am, and this job I love has taken a toll on me, my marriage, and my good standing in a company for which I've worked the majority of my career."

"What can I do for you, Luc?"

Lucas ignores the offer.

"Gordon, tomorrow you will stalk your buff and I will follow you. I have to warn you of one thing, though."

"What's that, Lucas?"

After another thoughtful pause Lucas looks at his friend and client and says,

"If you screw this up and get yourself hurt, I'll have to kill you and bury you in an antbear hole!"

They both laugh and Gordon is relieved he'll get to hunt his way and he promises that if he dies Lucas can dispose of his body any way he wishes.

The cook opens a bottle of Pinotage, serves grilled impala chops, and roasted pumpkin with butter and cinnamon, and with their negotiations behind them they toast the moment, they toast Africa, and they toast tomorrow.

They eat happily with their new treaty confirmed, drink until they both are slightly silly, and then retire early to get the rest they'll need for tomorrow's walking. As Gordon lies awake, he thinks about the stresses a PH endures. He thinks about Luc and Lise, their marriage, and the penance Lise endures while she watches her husband work more, eat more, drink more, and care about their relationship less. Lucas is so focused on providing for Lise he has lost sight of what she really needs from him. Gordon's mind swims in the muck of it all until it distresses his heart. Then his mind reminds him he has no business in Africa except with a Cape buffalo, so he falls asleep seeing Dagga Boys wallowing in the mud because that's what his mind wanted.

On Their Own

A s the sun breaks the horizon, the Askari realizes what it is to be alone. For a herd animal, this is a hard new reality. He's never been nor ever wanted to be alone. He wonders what it would be like to be a solitary animal like a leopard or a bushbuck. What a lonely existence that would be, he needs his family. He remembers what the Dagga Boy said about lessons; this one will never leave him. An impala ram bursts the quiet with rutting barks while sprinting through the bushveld in wide circles, chasing off other rams. He pushes the other impala rams to the outside and at the same time corrals the ewes in.

The Dagga Boy, resting but not asleep, cracks a dry eyelid and exclaims, "Impalas! Everyone in the bush has to know when the impalas are in the rut. Just because their ewes are in heat we have to put up with that persistent, hyperventilative barking from those idiots. They don't even fight like other animals. They take their delicate little horns, and their delicate little hooves and push each other back and forth a few times, and then they run in circles barking incessantly, shouting about their dominance over one another.

A buff, Askari, need not tell the entire bushveld who's in charge. By his fighting and his fidelity to the herd, all will know."

"Dagga Boy," says Askari, "we have to find water. It's been a day and I'm beginning to dry from the inside."

Dagga Boy reflectively says, "It may be my last dry season and it seems to be one of the worst I can recall. I won't miss the dry seasons, especially the hard ones like this. Push your hoof into the mud, Askari, water may rise into the depression. Sometimes it's enough to wet your mouth, sometimes your throat too, and sometimes it's enough for a few swallows."

The Askari does as he's told but the water is only enough to make the mud glisten like fresh scat, nothing more. The Dagga Boy sees before the Askari says a word and begins to walk.

"There's a water hole I remember not too far from here," says the old Dagga Boy, "but we have to cross roads to get to it. The danger in crossing the roads is the hunters will find your tracks and follow you from behind. But if you can keep the wind at your back, and your eyes ahead, you'll be safe from two directions. Just remember to check your backtrack. The breeze can be deceiving. Then, when we're near the water, we'll make a wide circle and come to it with our faces in the wind so if the hunters are following us we will have all of our senses toward them. When we stop to rest we will lay back to back, and when we walk it will be very slowly, side by side, so it is no good to shoot at either one of us. The impalas will follow us because they need the water too, but they're stupid because of the rut and we can use them to get there safely."

Gordon Takes the Lead

*W*ith Lucas at the wheel and Gordon beside him, the Land Rover crawls the along the desiccated red clay roads. The trackers are on the high bench in the bed of the truck, surveying the bushveld as they go. The transmission sounds like a coffee grinder and Gordon wonders out loud about the four of them carrying a buff back to camp.

"These old Rovers never die," Lucas says. "As long as I keep a few tools in the glove box and a roll of baling wire in the back, we won't have any trouble."

"Maybe it's just the threat of you working on it that keeps it going," Gordon jokes as he twists a knuckle, imitating a ratchet, into Lucas's ribcage.

"Feeling pretty good about yourself today, aren't you?"

"As a matter of fact, I am. Find me some tracks and let me go. The way I see it, we've made several failed stalks on several small herds. Now let's say we have eight buffs, that is sixteen eyes, ears, and nostrils all tuned to detecting predators like us. That's forty-eight chances to bust any one of the four of us, and sometimes,

Lucas," he throws in for effect, "you and the trackers could use a little extra bathing if you know what I mean. That gives me about a one in one hundred ninety-two chance for success. So let's say that we reduce the number of buffs to four, a small group of old Dagga Boys, you know, and then we reduce the number of humans to one, virtually odor free, super stalking, bow building, one-thousand-grain arrow shooting, hunter like me. The odds give me a one in twenty-four chance of going home with my buff."

"Yeah, and if we find a half-blind Dagga Boy asleep in the mud you can stone him to death, too! Your chances are slimmer than you think, my friend, but if your vision of how this day unfolds comes true we'll be barbequing buffalo back straps and I'll be one very happy PH at sundown."

"Yes, my friend, it's going to be a good sundown."

Gordon's excitement and his insecurity fight for control of him and he realizes the seriousness of what he's finally gotten the chance to do. He recognizes now is the time to shut his mouth and open his eyes.

Dagga Boy and the Lions

" *H*ow did you save us from that lion attack, Dagga Boy?" the Askari asks. "I was young, they kept me to the inside of the herd, and I couldn't see anything at all".

"You remember that?" says Dagga Boy proudly. "I'll tell you the story but keep walking and keep your senses about you, we may see hunters near the road."

He begins the story. "It was nightfall and we knew the lions were near the water where we were headed. Lions have a smell easy for a buff to recognize. Meat eaters smell differently from grazers. The herd needed water and sometimes you have to take chances. So the lions let us drink and get somewhat comfortable before they started for us. The pride queen was scanning us for an opportunity; we knew the attack was coming. The air was thick with tension. Slowly we buffs gathered you young ones to the inside and began a retreat but they followed and started darting inside our perimeter to get a calf to break to the outside. All of the buffs were calling out, panicked at the attack. But panic kills, Askari, so when things go bad, don't panic. The lionesses had no intention of giving up so I decided, at that very moment, the only good lion is a dead lion. If they were going to take one from my herd then I would kill as many of them as I could for payment and make them remember my herd and me for the trouble we gave them. I maneuvered to the back and when I had the attention of the queen I broke free and charged hard right, away from the herd. The queen thundered down on me bringing her sisters and daughters and she leapt upon my back. The rest of them were clawing at my flanks while she was pulling her way up toward my neck. The inexperienced girls ran at my rear hooves and it only took a few well-timed kicks to be rid of them. The ones flanking me were the hardest because I couldn't get a kick into them and they were trying to attach to my legs and hips to bring me down where they could all pile upon my throat at the same time. I had to keep running long enough for the queen to reach my head where she could make her final assault on me. She clawed her way up my spine sinking them into my flesh and pulling forward as I ran. She squared both paws at my shoulders and pulled hard one last time to get to my neck. She looked down at my head searching for that soft part of throat just behind the jaws where she could collapse my windpipe or rupture my carotid artery. Then all she would have to endure is a few last front kicks from a half dead buff whose demise was certain before feeding her pride. I held my chin low to the ground, my ears pounded with adrenaline, and my bosses ached to collide with her face. As she lunged down for the kill I threw them back as hard as I could."

"What happened?" Askari asks, amazed at the story.

"Keep your eyes open and your nose to the air and I'll finish. The momentum was too much for the lioness' jaw to absorb, and I felt it collapse completely as I heard the sounds of bone and teeth fracture into useless pieces. The rest of her weight fell onto my neck and I rolled my horns sideways embedding a curl just behind her ear, and then came the sound."

"What sound, Dagga Boy?" asks the all-too-excited Askari.

"The sound of a lioness who couldn't control her voice because her jaw's hanging from her face, her ears are ringing so loud from pain that she can't hear herself, the terror that comes from not knowing where her pride is, the air being forced out her lungs when she hits the ground, and the awareness only that she can no longer breathe because the muscles around her back and rib-cage have constricted so tightly to protect themselves from further harm that they aren't letting any air in. It was a sound that told everyone who could hear it, that, at that moment, she would rather be dead than alive."

"Did she die, Dagga Boy?"

"She did die, Askari, but she didn't die then. She rolled on the ground reeling in her agony. The sounds she made told her pride that something was very wrong, and they left me to tend to their matron. Lions, you see, don't understand not being in control of any and every situation. They'll stop in a moment of confusion to regain order and that is when they lose.

"That old lioness suffered for weeks with bleeding gums and a useless jaw. Unable to eat, she grew weaker and weaker until her pride abandoned her. She eventually realized her fate to a pack of hyenas."

Using the Impala

"Askari, slow down."

"Are you tired, Dagga Boy? Should we rest?"

"No, I'm not tired," Dagga Boy scolds but thinking, *I'm exhausted.* He adds another lesson in his reply to the youngster.

"We're getting close to the road, Askari, we need to let the impalas catch up to us."

"But why, Dagga Boy? They're idiots."

"Yes, Askari, and that is why we must let them catch us. If we slow down they'll feed past us, and at the road they'll make many tracks and stir up a lot of dust. Our tracks will mix with theirs, and the dust will settle on top of the whole lot. The impala rams will come last, chasing each other, barking and carrying on, and stir the whole thing up again. If the hunters are good they'll still notice our tracks, but the mess made by the impalas will give us a chance that they won't."

The buffalos slow and then cross just behind the impala ewes. They walk slow and soft, and then, just as Dagga Boy predicted, the impala rams come. They chase each other relentlessly through and around the other tracks making a mess of the whole crossing. Their rut barks amuse Askari because he knows the reason they're so intoxicated even though he has yet to achieve that milestone of life. Beyond the road and safe in the cover of the veld, Dagga Boy stops for a rest. He has to remind Askari to lie with him back to back.

"I can still smell, Askari, and you've got eyes and ears far better than I do. Lie back to back with me and we can cover the whole area."

Breech of Trust

*T*he Rover motors down the red clay path with Lucas and Gordon scanning their respective sides for movement or color in the otherwise lifeless, gray bushveld. Gordon, connecting with his inner, ancestral bush bowman turns and leans over his seat to the rear seat area of the double cab to retrieve his face paint and go full Indian. Lucas's .500 nitro double is sandwiched between the fleece vests, nylon lunch coolers, and extra boots, and as Gordon fishes through his pack he feels an urge from within. He locks his eyes onto the break action rifle. He knows he wants to finish this hunt his way, no rifle, no back up. He puts his hand on the breech cupping his palm over the top to muffle the noise, his thumb finds the release lever and as Lucas shifts down into second gear, the truck whines. Gordon prods the lever sideways exposing the two index finger sized cartridges. He can't believe what he's doing. His mind races from safety to betrayal to the unwritten law of touching the gun, bow, knife, or dog of another man without asking. The truck bogs into sand and Gordon panics but slides the two cartridge ends alternating between three fingers of his left hand and slips them free of the barrels. He closes the action, checks to make sure the safety is on, and slips the cartridges into the inside pocket of his pack.

A sharp whistle from Daniel and the truck stops abruptly. Gordon falls back to the front seat snagging the face paint and Lucas says, "Welcome back, Gordon, we have tracks. What were you doing back there?"

Gordon's heart stops and lacking any breath at all, he simply holds up the tin of camo face paint.

"Well, put your makeup on, we've got work to do," Lucas says and steps out of the truck as he starts speaking fast in Afrikaans. The gravity of what Gordon has done pounds at his chest, but before he loses control, he repeats his longbow mantra to himself,

Stalk slow, low, mind the wind, and get close. Forget the heart, nothing lives without lungs. Anchor, focus, nothing moves when you release.

Daniel steps from behind the truck, Gordon sees the back of the black T-shirt he's wearing which, in over-sized white block lettering, reads L'Oreal Paris. Gordon looks at the tracker's bald black head and the lean body and jokes to Lucas that they're hunting with a male supermodel, and they both chuckle relieving some of Gordon's anxiety.

After a rapid-fire discussion in Afrikaans, Lucas turns to Gordon and says,

"You're a lucky man today, my friend, we have two buffs alone. It looks like a Dagga Boy and an Askari. If we play our cards correctly, you may get a shot."

Lucas slips the rifle out of its soft surroundings and cradles it just in front of the trigger guard in his left hand. He unsnaps the leather cartridge wallet on his belt and Gordon can't breathe as Lucas thumbs the two empty sheaths inside the carrier and then counts the four remaining cartridges by sliding his thumb across their tops.

One, two, three, four, and two in the chambers I loaded this morning, Lucas thinks.

He checks the safety, lifts the double rifle to his shoulder holding it just behind the muzzle, and walks to the spoor crossing the road. Daniel parks the truck out of plain view and all four converge at the roadside. Lucas takes the lead and Gordon gives a short, sharp whistle imitating Daniel.

"What?" asks Lucas.

"Remember our deal? I'll be taking the lead on this one, my good man. Let Daniel walk up front with me until we're near the buffs, then I'll break solo."

Gordon and Daniel take to each side of the tracks and Daniel carefully points out the large buff tracks, the smaller buff tracks, and those of the impalas. Every twenty meters or so, Daniel stubs his toe into the red clay releasing a small cloud of fine dust that drifts in the almost undetectable breeze, checking the wind. The moving is slow and deliberately quiet. Lucas is especially quiet, not happy as a spectator.

Getting Old

"What's the worst part about getting old, Dagga Boy?"

"My hips hurt whether I'm standing or lying down. My eyes see the color of milk in front of everything I look at. My teeth are rotting out of my head so that it's getting harder every day to eat, and my mouth tastes of those rotting teeth constantly."

"What's the best part of getting old?"

The old bull ponders the moment and then answers, "Teaching you young bulls to save yourselves from the dangers of the bush and how to manage a herd. I hope I've been a good example and my herd continues to be led from within, Askari. I'd hate it if some rogue bulls from outside the herd took over. There's also a satisfaction that I've defeated all of the hunters and all of the lions that have come for me. Just living to be my age is an accomplishment for a buff."

At that thought, the Dagga Boy gets up with a great effort to get his own weight off of the ground and Askari follows without asking why. They begin toward the water, the impalas now far ahead of them. They walk on, following the tracks of the impalas through the spotted brush of the bushveld until the Askari sees the impala ewes gathered shoulder to shoulder at the water far ahead.

"There it is, Dagga Boy, the water and the impalas," exclaims Askari.

"Yes it is, but this is not the time to be stupid, Askari. Many animals get shot heading to the water because their senses are lost to their thirst."

"What will we do?"

Dagga Boy offers another lesson to the young policeman, how to enter waterholes safely.

"Askari, what we need to do is head wide north around the water and far past it. Eyes and ears open, Askari, and nose to the breeze. The impalas will stay at the water until we get there, the rams have pushed the ewes hard and they all need their fill. We will walk until we're far past the water, then turn back and come into the wind as we walk to it. If there's trouble the impalas will know, maybe one will get shot, and then we just wait until it's carted off before we go in and drink. The impalas are dumb during their rut, but they scare easily. Watch them closely, Askari."

"What if our tracks are seen on the road, Dagga Boy?"

The old bull answers, "Just keep checking our back trail. If there are hunters following, they're very unlikely to shoot us from the rear on the first shot. They won't get to the water without upsetting the impalas so we'll know that too. We'll keep our course, slow and cautious and get to the water safe, not fast."

The Dung Hunter's Plan

ordon, Lucas, and the two trackers softly walk the tracks of the buffs, keeping all eyes ahead for movement or color. They find new buff dung and Gordon stops to look. Squatting to get closer, he sets down his bow and removes his shooting glove. He picks up a handful of the dung and wrings the juices out onto his boots. A second handful gets both boots soaked and he rubs them until the liquid soaks into the leather. The remainder of the dung he begins to work into his pants, starting at the shins and working up to his crotch, and then two more handfuls go around his collar and under his arms. When he's finished, he wipes his hands clean on the front of his shirt. He looks up to see the trackers watching him with big wide toothy grins but Gordon can't tell if they think he's the dumbest or the smartest hunter they've ever hunted with, or just comically stupid. Gordon thinks how funny it is that one expression could mean totally opposite things. He can't figure out if the trackers are laughing inside at him, if they're nervous because they think he's gone crazy and if they don't show approval they'll receive the wrath of his insanity, or if they really do approve and support the dung bathing. It doesn't really matter what they think of him, except that he does respect them and their abilities as trackers and given the chance, he thinks they would be hunters to marvel at, especially Daniel. Whether the trackers are expressing fear, disapproval, or support, Gordon is in one of the best moments of his life and he intends to do it his way.

"You don't expect the rest of us to do that, do you?" Lucas asks.

"There's not enough dung in the bushveld to cover your stink, Lucas. You'd gag a buzzard off a gut wagon."

Then Gordon winks at the trackers, which causes them to stretch their grins just a little further. He begins to walk again until they find the two large orbs in the dirt indicating the old Dagga Boy needed a rest.

"He's an old one," Lucas says, "He had to rest before the water."

"Or he's a smart one," Gordon replies. "It may be that he needed time to think more than rest. If he really is a big, old Dagga Boy, he didn't get that way by being stupid. He could have stopped to let the impala go first so they'd get shot instead of him."

Lucas says, "Good thought, dung hunter. What's your next move?"

"Don't know yet. Maybe we should follow on slowly for a while."

"It's your day, Gordon, but I'll caution you, we'll only get one chance at a Dagga Boy. He won't let us chase him around the bushveld all day. As soon as he figures out we're on his trail, he'll be gone. One more thing, Gordon, the water is just ahead."

Gordon begins to realize that out of the four men present, he's the absolute least experienced Cape buffalo hunter, and he's now, by the liberation of his own ego, put himself in charge of something he is the least qualified to lead. Hiding his newfound insecurity he slowly, carefully, tracks on looking more for inspiration than buff tracks. At the point where the buffs veered north, he stops.

"Where's the water, Lucas?"

Lucas answers, "Straight ahead, and before you ask, they turned north for one of two reasons. The first, they sensed danger at the water and abandoned it altogether. The second, he's making a wide circle around the water hole so he can come into it with his face in the wind. That old Dagga Boy's done this water dance thousands of times and, so far, has no holes in his hide. Best we can do now is keep tracking cautiously and hope we can catch him as he circles back. That is, unless you think you've got enough dung rubbed on you that you might walk straight into the water and wait for them."

Gordon thinks about the situation, ignoring the ridicule, and tries to get inside the mind of the Dagga Boy. He prays silently, not for killing the Dagga Boy, as it's just not good to pray for a kill. He prays just to do the right thing, just to make the next decision correctly. He tries to connect with his father who's twenty years dead this year but to whom he still talks frequently. The inspiration he's hoping to find doesn't find him. He turns to Lucas and says,

"All right, friend, you go first."

Lucas turns to the trackers. Speaking in Afrikaans, he tells them to go to the truck and wait. Gordon gets a wink and a gesture of releasing an arrow from Daniel and the two leave without a word. The simple gesture makes Gordon realize that Daniel's hoping to see what a man with a wood bow can do against a Cape buffalo, and that he's hoping for Gordon's success. Maybe it's just that primal instinct that all hunters share, regardless of their place of birth, their color, or status in their community. All hunters share something inside their souls that excites them to the core. This one simple gesture animates Gordon and gives him confidence. It inspires a thought and a plan to bring this stalk to the Dagga Boy.

"You ready now, Gordon, slow and easy, and follow me." Lucas says going back into PH mode.

"Well, my friend," Gordon responds, "I've got a different idea. I'd like *you* to follow north around the water, keeping to the buff tracks."

"Would you like me to shoot him for you, too?" Lucas asks, not quite sure what's come over his friend. Gordon stares at Lucas, offended by the remark. Lucas searches Gordon's eyes in the silence.

He wonders if Gordon's scared. He's had many scared clients. He wonders if Gordon's lost faith in himself, having seen it happen to many hunters. Gordon, on the other hand, wonders what Lucas's going to do when he tells him he wants to hunt this buff solo, but he feels like it's the only way to bring this to a good end.

Gordon breaks the silence. "I'm headed south around the water, Lucas, stay on the tracks and follow them. See if you can get them in your binoculars and stay with them but don't let them know you're there, and don't get any closer than seventy-five meters from the water."

He picks up a thorn and draws in the red clay the shape of a heart with a small circle in it. The circle represents the water hole and the heart halves being the north and south paths the two men are about to take. The obvious ridicule would have been easy, but Lucas sees the plan and really understands the merit of what Gordon's proposing.

Gordon continues, "I'll circle around from the south and head into the water as they do the same from the north, and if this all comes together I'll get broadside to them at shooting distance and all you'll have to do is watch."

"You realize this plan leaves you unprotected with me so far away," Lucas says, "and if you get yourself killed there will be a big stink and it'll fall right on me."

"Sure, I know, but there's only one thing going to die today, and it ain't me. You can shoot a buff from that distance with the .500, I'm sure of that Lucas. Just be ready and watch the whole thing over your front sight. One more thing, Lucas, don't you shoot my buff, please, don't shoot my buff."

With a smirk, Lucas replies, "Me shooting your buff depends upon you shooting your buff, and we're a long way from worrying about that now. Do this good, my friend, and I won't have to."

With Lucas signing off on the plan, Gordon wastes no time in leaving him, heading on a southern path around the water hole. He circles slow and wide, keeping low beneath the bushes, standing only to glass for his bearing and to check for animals. Being on his own in the bush is captivating and Gordon feels the need to stop for just a moment and pray.

"Heavenly Father, thank you for this day and for the opportunity just to be in this wonderful place, if nothing at all happens today I'm so grateful just to be here anyway. Lastly, Father, bless Lucas, keep him safe and help him understand someday why I did what I have done to him."

With this Gordon stretches his back and rolls his head in a slow clockwise motion then snaps his chin upward sharply making two vertebrae in his neck pop. The release of pressure makes him feel good. He takes a peek over the top of the brush before walking on at a low crouch, weaving between the bushes and trying not to make contact so their tops don't rustle.

An impala sounds in the distance and the grunts get closer, so close that Gordon lies flat in the dirt. The ram runs by close enough that Gordon can hear the thud of his hooves on the red clay. He smiles at his little victory (not being seen by the impala), and as he gets back to his feet he slides his right hand into the outside pocket of his pack and fingers the small grunt call that's been there for years without fail. He pulls it out, slips the lanyard over his head, slides the call between the top two buttons of his shirt and walks on.

Lucas makes time on his track and soon catches movement through the binoculars. He sees the two buffs but can't make out the horns. He walks on further north so the wind doesn't carry his scent down over the backs of the buffs but keeps the pair in sight with his binoculars. He sees only brief glimpses of shoulder and horn, or sometimes the swat of a tail as the buffs move through the brush. He's a hundred meters from the buffalos, confident he can make up the ground he'll need to put himself in shooting position once they circle and head up wind. He feels secure that he'll be able to protect his client, his friend, and that Gordon may get his buff after all. Lucas slows to a very quiet, heel-to-toe walk, and glasses for Gordon but can't find him. He's not concerned, as Gordon and he know each other, trust each other, and wouldn't be together now if they didn't like and respect each other. They'll meet at the water, Lucas from the north, Gordon from the south. Buff or not, all will be good.

All Askaris Fail

Dagga Boy breaks the silence as the two buffs walk together.

"Askari, we need to circle wide now and get directly downwind of the water. You keep your eyes open and remember, walk side by side."

"Good, Dagga Boy, I'm ready for water. I'll keep us safe, my eyes are sharp, my ears and nose ready to find anything human. It's my job to protect you and I intend to, Dagga Boy, I'll keep you safe."

"Your job is also to learn my lessons, Askari, just remember what I've shown you and what I've told you. Some day I will die, but not today, I'm old, Askari, and when your eyes are cloudy, your teeth are rotten, your ears deceive you, and your hips strain to bear your own weight, as a buff you've lived a good long life. Eventually, just living becomes a great struggle. I'm tired, Askari, and when animals and humans are near the end of their lives and they can admit that they're tired it means that they've accepted and made peace with dying. The relief that comes from accepting dying makes the mind and the heart light, if nothing else."

"You're not dying any time soon, and you're not dying on my watch. I'm not going back to the herd a failed Askari because my Dagga Boy, the greatest herd bull our herd has ever had, got killed with me as his Askari!"

The old buff calmly explains to his young apprentice, "Listen to me, all Askaris fail, and there is nothing you or I can do about it. Even if the best happens and we can keep away from the hunters, I will grow too weak to travel, then too weak to eat, then too weak too even stand and when that happens it will be impossible for you to keep the lions off me. They'll take this old defenseless Dagga Boy with their numbers, each one holding a leg and the merciful ones on the throat, one closing my wind and another searching for the place to release my blood. When this happens, Askari, you must let it happen because, if you don't, you will only prolong my pain. If the hunters get the better of us before the lions, you must let me handle that too. All herd animals sacrifice, it's something you must realize. You always minimize the loss to your herd, Askari. You have to know when to let go, and when to save yourself and your herd. You must survive, Askari, you are the future of my herd."

"What do you mean, Dagga Boy?"

"It is why you were chosen my Askari, it is why I've given you my lessons. In another season you will be the herd bull, and you will be for several years to come. Many will challenge you but just remember, Askari, remember these days with me and remember that every challenge contains a lesson."

Askari has no idea how to answer Dagga Boy so he says nothing at all but thinks about the future, the past, and the lessons.

Treachery Begets Treachery

*G*ordon begins a wide sweep to put himself directly downwind of the water hole. He hasn't glassed the buffs yet but he has a quiet confidence that he's, so far, done everything he can to put himself broadside to a buff.

A branch wedges between his bow limb and string and pulls backward at the longbow as he walks. He turns to look and gives the bow an instinctive pull, which causes the rest of the branch to sweep his face, and a thorn drives into his temple. It pulls like a dull knife above his eyebrow to the middle of his forehead and his head bleeds immediately.

"That was the second dumbest thing you've done today," Gordon says softly to himself.

He works first to free the bow and then releases himself from the briar. He pulls the old cotton bandana he wears on his head down a little to absorb the blood and wipes his brow clean with his

163

sleeve. He smiles at his new pain because sometimes pain is funny, and wonders why head wounds bleed so much and always seem worse than they really are. With the blood and the briar dealt with, Gordon glasses the bushveld again. Again, he sees nothing so he walks on.

Lucas sees the buffs complete their turn and watches as they head into the wind. He's north and west of the buffs so they'll have to pass directly south of him to reach the water hole. Sometime between now and then he hopes to see Gordon, whom he imagines is crawling on his belly across the bushveld. Lucas thinks about traditional bowhunters and how dedicated they are to doing things their own way. It's very hard to work with them and the limitations of their equipment, but because of the limitations they accept for themselves, it makes it hard not to admire them. All the animals they take are trophies, even rabbits and partridges. They're very simple in that respect.

He pans his binoculars from the buffs to the water and checks the disposition of the impala. They seem calm for impala, which are never really calm. This is good for him, for Gordon, and for the buffs. He pans back toward the buffs and before he gets there he sees a disturbance in the bush that he hopes is his hunter. He looks on, trying to make out the source of the movement in the bush but can't. He knows it is Gordon though, and begins to whisper to him hoping, subliminally, he'll get the instructions.

"That's it, Gordy boy, don't get too far north or you'll be in their wind. Just stay put and let them pass. Then you can quarter in from behind when you have the wind. Quarter in and take one, either one, any buff's a trophy with a longbow. Don't be stupid now, Gordy, we're almost home. I'm moving in now to set up for a shot. You get that arrow in his lungs proving you killed him; I'll break his back and then put one in the base of his skull so he doesn't kill you. You'll be livid at me but when you see your buff, you'll forgive me, you'll have to."

Lucas moves in slow but excited, like when he's hunting for himself. He gains a good position to shoot from, as the buffs get closer. He finds a small termite mound and takes his hand and rubs a cradle into the top of it for his rifle. He settles in behind now confident in the hide, the gun rest, and his decision to pick them.

Gordon stretches upward from a crouch to glass, and before he raises his binoculars he sees two large Cape buffalo north and just upwind, almost at shooting distance.

How did that happen? he thinks as he ducks down low.

He slips off his pack and quiver and then raises the strap of his quiver back over his head, and as he does this he slips one arrow free and holds the arrow and the bow in his left hand. He crawls toward the buffs as they move toward the water. On hands and knees he moves on quietly, slowly, like the grazing animals. He goes to predator mode, his movements becoming fluid and less mechanical. Reaching forward, right hand then left hand; a step forward, right knee then left knee; then a pause and repeat. Gordon slowly gains ground on the buffs trying not to notice their horns or evaluate the bosses and the curls. He reassures himself as he crawls.

Doing good, old boy, take the ground when you can. If you can get at them before they reach the clearing at the water they'll never see you.

At that he reaches forward with his left hand and as he bears his weight on it a thorn pierces the web between two fingers. He sucks in a sharp breath with the pain and doubles over to balance on his knees. Askari catches the sound of Gordon's panicked breath and the flipping of the bush tops where he's kneeling.

"Stop, Dagga Boy, there's trouble behind us," Askari warns in a panic. Dagga Boy turns to focus and sees the last wavering of the bush tops before they go still. Gordon sees the pair's sudden stop and their strain to find the danger they expect is coming. He pulls the thorn with his teeth and lets it fall to the ground and then pulls the grunt call from his shirt. Still doubled over Gordon risks everything.

He blows the grunt call in rapid repetition like the rut-inspired impala rams, hoping to fool the buffs. Just for effect he thrashes the brush around him with his bow limbs. The buffs stare and Gordon holds still again waiting for their decision.

"Impalas," Dagga Boy says, "they can startle you when your mind is focused on other things."

"I didn't see horns. I don't like this, Dagga Boy, and they're always running when they bark."

Dagga Boy reminds Askari that even the small rams will bark during the rut just to prove their relevance, even though they have no relevance at all.

"We probably spooked him and he had to bark at us even though he's running away. Come, Askari, the water's close, my mouth is dry".

The old bull turns his attention toward the water and the young bull reluctantly follows. Gordon finally exhales, and with the buffs' heads turned away, he continues his crawl. Making time and ground on them he begins to think of passing them and angling up to hide behind a thornbush and lie in wait for them.

The buffalos, now set on water, are between Gordon and Lucas. The two walk side by side, the Dagga Boy to Lucas' side and the Askari to the side of Gordon. Lucas, already in shooting position, has time to study the big buff.

What a champion, he thinks, *I'd shoot him myself and never want another.*

Gordon slowly overtakes the cautious buffs but remains well south of them. He stops on his knees beside a scrub on the edge of the clearing to the water. He's still twenty yards south of their path. He thinks about the bushveld and how there's possibly not a better place on earth to stalk game. There are a few impalas remaining at the water but most have moved on. Gordon thinks about the buffs coming toward him and the last few impalas he'll have to manage if he's going to get a shot. He thinks about the position he's taken for the buffs, and though he'd like to be just a bit closer, he thinks he's far enough to shoot from cover and avoid a charge. Then he thinks about what he did to Luc but quickly puts that thought away. Right or wrong, you can't change the past, only affect the future, and the immediate future needs his focus for his own sake and for Lucas'.

Gordon sees the buffs in brief glimpses as they pass from bush to bush, and realizes the young Askari is on his side. He doesn't mind at all because the plan, the stalk, and the shot, are all that matter. Trophy size is no matter now as he's already, in his mind, successful. Stalking to twenty yards from two good Cape buffalo with a longbow is a great achievement, and for a moment, a fraction of a second, he's overcome with the excitement of his circumstance. The buffs steadily make for the water, Lucas finds Gordon in the binoculars, and Gordon removes the remaining two arrows from his quiver and places them quietly to the ground next to him.

Lucas raises the butt of the rifle to his shoulder and squares the sights to his eye. His focus is the large buff on his side as all he can see of the other is the legs. He scans the Dagga boy for spots of aim, the spine, the shoulder, and he even looks at the hips thinking, worst case, two shots from the double .500 may shatter the hips of the bull rendering him useless to charge. He slows his breathing and maps the scene for Gordon, the buffs, and their future paths. He rubs the trigger guard with his index finger and inhales as he catches the smell of the gun oil. It gives him a sense of belonging, a feeling that he's at the place that best fits him. He hugs the grip with his thumb and three remaining fingers to reassure the rifle that he's at the ready or to reassure himself there's nothing at all changed in their relationship, and the two wait to do the thing they do together most well.

Into the Open

"Before you step into the open, Askari, stop and use every sense you have," the old bull warns. "Look at the bush all around the water, smell the air long, and point your ears in every direction. Then I want you to walk directly to the water, take as much as you can, and get back to the bush. If it's safe we may wait until dark and try it again. If no lions come, we will have our fill."

"All right, Dagga Boy, follow me."

Dagga Boy scolds, "No! Side by side, Askari, hunters won't shoot if we're side by side. When the herd is together you can send a younger bull in first. If he gets shot, the herd's safe and you've survived. Save the females for breeding and growing the herd. When there are only two, you go in together, side by side."

The Askari, taking his job very seriously, does as the Dagga Boy instructs, checking the wind, turning his ears to all directions, and scanning the bush. When he feels it is safe, the two buffs step out into the open and make for the water.

Uuuurp, the grunt call breaks the silence. Gordon spits it out while drawing the string to the corner of his mouth. The Askari stops abruptly, startled, and he flinches as the few remaining impalas at the water explode. The old Dagga Boy knows the noise, this time, is no impala. He knows he's been caught broadside by a hunter, and he knows it's time to take control of his own ending. He is tired and he no longer has the will to run, and he knows Askari must survive.

He takes two steps forward, passing Askari by half a length. He extends his foreleg forward exposing his final gift to the herd, his final lesson to Askari, and, his great heart. He makes out through clouded eyes the shape of the bent limbs of a wood bow and the camouflaged mound of a hunter kneeling behind them. The old bull is satisfied that this hunter is, above all, fair and good, and that this, finally, is a proper way to die. For a moment, there is no sound.

Fffit, the string splits the air and the arrow flies seemingly in slow motion from Gordon's perspective. The Dagga Boy sees the flash of the broadhead and braces for the impact. His rib splits as the shaft drives through his chest leaving nothing exposed but the arrow's white feathers on the black background of his body.

Lucas' first shot results in what he thinks is a misfire as the gun makes a "clack" of metal on metal with nothing in front of the firing pin. His finger quickly finds the rear trigger and squeezes as the front sight settles on the spine of the old bull. "Clack" again and Lucas realizes something has gone terribly, maybe fatally wrong.

"AAAAAH!" Lucas screams to avert the buffalo's attention from his hunter to himself. He charges them as he breaks the rifle open with his left hand and tries to manipulate two new shells from the wallet on his right hip. His body finds, for a short burst, the faster, more powerful legs of the younger rugger he used to be.

Askari yells, "Right side, Dagga Boy!" as he turns to face Lucas.

Dagga Boy keeps his hooves firmly anchored but turns to see Lucas and tells Askari, "Run, son, run and don't look back. Find the herd, Askari, it's yours now."

Lucas looks down at the chambers of the rifle and becomes painfully struck with panic finding them empty. His mind races for reasons from subterfuge by his friend Gordon, a grave mistake on his own part, or incompetence of the trackers. As he runs it becomes clear that he is failing. He can't run and manipulate the cartridges from the bouncing wallet on his belt with any dexterity and if he stops to load, the few seconds that it will take will allow the buff and Gordon to decide the ending without him, which is never the choice of a PH. A Professional Hunter is, above all else, supposed to be in control at all times. The gun, the buffs, the almost- sure-to-be-dead hunter, and his own adrenaline send him to maximum stress. Stopping now means only being a spectator, so he runs.

The Dagga Boy stands watching Lucas, knowing that the second arrow is soon to come. Another rib splinters and for a moment Dagga Boy closes his eyes to help absorb the burn as the second shaft chisels into the far shoulder just above the first. Askari makes for the safety of the bushveld and leaves Gordon and the old Dagga Boy to finish their business. Dagga Boy turns to face Gordon and collects the adrenaline for one last charge, his lungs filling with blood but his legs feeling surprisingly strong. Gordon stands to face the bull, and to make sure it doesn't charge Lucas. He nocks his final arrow. With nowhere to run and no trees to climb he has to finish this Dagga Boy alone, the way he'd always seen it in his mind. Taking a breath and raising his bow arm he sees the blood foaming out of the Dagga Boy's chest. He knows the bull is done and he needs just to survive the time until the bull's body realizes it. Dagga Boy raises his great head for the charge and for the first time Gordon sees the mass of the bosses and curls. He hooks three fingers on the string and as he draws it to the corner of his mouth, his world becomes silent as his mind takes control. His mind knows his sight is the most important sense, so it shuts the others down. As Dagga Boy raises his head for the charge, Gordon sees the buff's throat blending down to a massive chest and knows there's no shot to be had that will affect this outcome. His only chance is to wait. His only last shot at the Dagga Boy has to be in the spine when the bull lowers its head for impact. It's either that or run like hell, and he, like the Dagga Boy, doesn't want to run from this.

The old bull lunges forward and the left foreleg snaps the arrow shafts sending the white, feathered pieces end over end into the air and out of Gordon's sight. Lucas stops to load and hammers the action closed. He shoulders the double and over the Dagga Boy's back he sees Gordon at full draw just beyond the bull. Lucas holds steady knowing the one thing that he doesn't want is a .500 nitro solid in his hunter. All the other problems he has at the moment, though difficult, could be explained to the authorities. A bullet in your client only gives a PH one result, and he's not yet ready to become a petrol jockey.

The Dagga boy's intentions are clear, to run right through Gordon. At the first stride the bull closes to fifteen yards, at the second he lowers his head for impact. Gordon finds the cervical spine just behind the head and releases the string. The arrow's speed and weight combined with the bull running toward the arrow in flight makes for magnificent momentum that, on the bull's third stride, severs his cervical spine just in front of the shoulders. Gordon stands, focused on the shot, and sees the front legs of the old bull buckle and collapse below his chest. The rear haunches fall behind the great body, the Dagga Boy's head bounces tethered to a lifeless neck, and then his muzzle hits the earth hard and skids, forcing the horns forward. The bosses collide with Gordon's shins sending both feet into the air behind him, and he tenses everything bracing for impact. Dagga Boy has a moment of clarity and realizes that he's pummeled his hunter, his killer. He has no pain at all and just as satisfaction arrives to the old boy his lungs release their air. A great mass of blood discharges from his mouth and nostrils, and he lies at peace, finally dead.

Gordon lands hard, his face into the buff's shoulders and feels the wind forced from him. His sinuses fill with the blood of a broken nose. His once silent ears begin to ring, and he feels pain from his face to his now throbbing shins.

Still holding the bow in his left hand he rolls off the buffalo's body and onto the hard, dry clay. As he pulls into the fetal position he catches just enough air to spit the blood out of the back of his sinuses, and begins the desperate, shallow breathing of having his wind knocked out.

Lucas gets to Gordon's side and after a quick jab to the Dagga Boy's eye to make sure he's dead says,

"Breathe, Gordon, it's over now, just breathe."

Lucas is calmly frantic as he performs triage on Gordon. He begins by rolling Gordon to his back, and then starts at the ankles and works his way up feeling for breaks and other trauma. He sees the mucous and blood still attached to the corner of Gordon's mouth by strings of spittle that lead to a puddle on the ground, and immediately thinks of broken ribs and punctured lungs.

He frantically yells into the radio for Daniel to bring the truck and then presses Gordon's ribs one by one convinced he'll find the one that was sacrificed to the bull. When Lucas reaches the top, Gordon, with breath finally captured, says,

"He broke my nose...not my ribs...quit groping me. He knocked the wind out of me...that's why I wasn't breathing."

Lucas smiles with relief, "You're lucky that's all he did."

Gordon adds to the sabotage of the gun by saying, "How come you didn't shoot?"

Lucas wonders if Gordon's playing a game of chess or if he's serious. He doesn't know where the question is leading him, and now he's doesn't know if Gordon knows about the gun or not. Gordon, feeling a bit like he's been hit by a train, really doesn't care what the answer is or if Lucas knows that he knows or not. A beating by Lucas now would surely be less noticed due to the current pain from the crash with the buff.

Lucas answers, "You said no guns, you're the boss today, remember?"

"Yes, yes, my friend, I do remember. I may have needed a hand, though."

Lucas, fishing for another answer and wishing the current topic to be over, says, "You seemed to have it all under control until you stood up, and when you did, you were in my line of fire."

Both wanting to move on to a different subject, Lucas extends a hand to Gordon, they clasp wrists, and Lucas pulls Gordon to his feet.

"Aaaaa, my shins!" Gordon yells.

He limps around in circles until his body realizes the shins aren't broken and the pain subsides somewhat. He walks to the place the Dagga Boy was standing when he took the first two arrows and finds the broken, fletched, pieces of arrow shaft and tucks them into his shirt pocket because they, in his mind, deserve not to be forgotten. He hobbles back to Lucas who is talking Afrikaans to the trackers. He tells them to relay a message to camp to bring an empty truck and all of the men they can find.

"He's a big Dagga Boy, a real champion, Gordon," Lucas says very quietly, very seriously, and very proud of his friend. Gordon looks at Lucas and says, "I think he committed suicide. The Askari stopped, and he just walked past him and stretched his front leg forward to give me his heart. It was like he didn't want to fight anymore."

"Look at him, his teeth are almost gone and his eyes are full of cataracts. He is very old Gordon. This Dagga Boy's escaped hunters, and lions, and has done it well to get this old. I don't think he'd just let you kill him if he could help it. He probably couldn't see you."

"I don't know, Lucas, it was almost like he was resigned to die. Like he was good with it, like he was ready, and like he wanted the young one to live. I was ready to take the Askari, and I'd have been thrilled with him, but then the old boy just pulled in front and exposed his heart to me. Something was very surreal about the whole thing, Luc. I think he knew what he was doing."

"Gordon, it was surreal for me, too. It was like a bad movie watching you do that on your own."

Lucas walks back for Gordon's pack and when he returns they sit, drinking water, and reflecting silently. They both think about the things that went well, the things that went badly, and the unanswered question.

"You shot that longbow well, friend, you scared me, but you shot well. Those first two were double-lung. If he didn't have so much adrenaline he would have died sooner. I bet if you had run hard after that he would have died before he caught you. You had a good lead on him."

"Thanks, Lucas, and thanks for letting me do it my way. I know you're liable for my safety, and I know you have VanZandt to answer to, and I do know that I can be a major pain in your rear. I appreciate you understanding my need to hunt on my own."

"You've been a pain in my rear since the day we met," Lucas jokes. "But I do admire the way you do things. Thank you, Gordon."

"For what?"

"For not getting yourself killed today, it would have been a mess for me to sort out."

"You'd have started by sorting through my wallet for sure."

"Small price to pay for the trouble you'd have left me."

They both smile and begin to relax in the fact that besides Gordon's broken nose, swollen shins, and being sore all over, there's nothing left to do but divide the meat and prepare the paperwork for the taxidermist.

The trackers drive in with a second truck and three more men from camp. Daniel shakes Gordon's hand so hard it makes his whole battered body hurt, but he tries not to let the pain show so he doesn't scare Daniel or spoil his good spirits. The celebration begins and they take dozens of photographs. Lucas, Gordon, Daniel, and other camp helpers, everybody wants pictures with the old Dagga Boy. Lucas and Gordon push aside their earlier thoughts and join the celebration. Everything has ended well and they've both, figuratively, dodged a bullet.

Living the Lie

$\mathcal{S}$itting at the fire pit, waiting for the sundowners to be served, Gordon remembers the events of the day over and over again and smiles through each scene. His only regret is the deception he committed upon his friend. If his pack was thrown in the front of the truck, if he'd put his face paint on in camp before they left, he would not have even thought of it, and it wouldn't have happened. Something about seeing the rifle lain across the coolers with such easy access made him — no, caused the idea — no, it was his fault, his responsibility and his alone. No matter how he was trying to justify it, he was wrong, and he knew he had to make it right.

Lucas is in the kitchen talking to Lise about the gun, the empty chambers, his guilt and how he endangered his client, his livelihood, and his family's security. Lise laughs at his last thought and says, "Security, what security? This is Africa, dear, and you're a PH. There is no security in the way that we live." A long pause separates the two into their own thoughts, then Lise offers, "We're all safe now and you can't change what happened, but if you're going to worry yourself to death you won't be any good to us, so just find a way to make it right."

Lucas thinks about all of the ways to tell Gordon, and all of the possible reactions he may get from him ranging from a laugh to a letter to the RSA Professional Hunter Licensing Review Board, which would surely lead to that alternative career at the petrol pumps. He thinks that maybe the trackers removed the shells the night before or for safety that morning while the gun was in the truck, and if he finds out if that's true, he'll surely hand out a few hidings to them. He is sure he loaded it just before they got in the truck this morning because even though they were just driving, he likes to have a loaded gun at the ready. He thinks again that Gordon may have done it, and the difficulty in handling a situation like that would be because it wouldn't be proper to give a client, especially a return client, a beating, or even one good fist to the face. Then he thinks about himself. Could he have forgotten to load the gun before they left this morning? And why didn't he check the chambers when he pulled the gun out of the truck. The self-doubt sets in. The cartridges were missing from his wallet. Where were they? No matter what really happened, not checking the gun when they left the truck made him feel the worst of all. If only he had checked before they started on the tracks. No matter how it happened, if he had checked, the gun would have been ready when he needed it. For this alone he feels the whole mess is his fault.

He kisses Lise and says, "I'll think of a way to make it right, but right now we better feed our hunter. He's had a day, playing rugby with a Dagga Boy."

He smiles and thinks of the beautiful simplicity in Lise's mind, and her "just make it right," when the complexity of the oversight is surely going to give him permanent anxiety. He leaves to check on Gordon at the fire and finds him wrapped in a fleece jacket, legs stretched straight out, and feet near the flames.

"Hey, bwanna, what can I get for you?"

Gordon's head is leaned back onto the reclined folding chair, his eyes are closed, and without opening them he says,

"I only need three things: a glass, three ice cubes, and two fingers of bourbon."

"Mind if I join you?"

Gordon smiles and says, "Wouldn't have it any other way, my friend, we started this together, let's finish it with a drink and another stunning African sunset."

Sipping their bourbon and starring at the fire, Lucas and Gordon sit quietly until a plate of biltong and fried grubs is set between them by one of Lise's helpers. Lucas picks out a fatty piece of meat, sets a grub on top, and puts them both in his mouth. Gordon's epicurean intrigue causes him to sandwich a grub between two slices of biltong, and pop it in his own mouth. He chews slowly trying to get the flavor of the fat, the dried flesh, and the chewy skin of the grub past the flavor of the bourbon. When he's satisfied he can't extract any more flavor from the food in his mouth he takes a sip of the bourbon and mixes it all before he swallows, leaving a greasy tongue and an aftertaste of salt and sweet corn liquor.

He says, "I could get used to this, you know. If I had any money left, I'd stay all season."

Lucas breathes in a slow sip of his bourbon and answers, "We still have the morning, what do you want to do?"

"Sleep, my whole body hurts and I think I'd rather have my face fall off than stay on. All I want to do is enjoy this bourbon with you, eat dinner, put some ice on my face, and sleep."

Lucas laughs and says, "You're pretty beat up. I thought we might shoot some hares before you leave. Just walk the bushveld, stalk pigs, hares, partridges, and guineas, like old times."

"Take Daniel with you, Luc. He'd love to go."

"He hunts all the time now."

"Really?"

"After he saved everybody last year, VanZandt lets him shoot all of the camp meat. He hunts more than I do."

"That's great Luc, I'll have to start sending him arrows."

"He'd love that, Gordon. He takes such good care of all of that gear you gave him."

"I'm so glad, Luc. I'm so glad for him."

Gordon closes his eyes again and smiling says, "It is fun having nothing else to do but walk and see what's hidden in the bush. It really makes me feel like a kid."

They drift into another pause in their conversation thinking about the previous trips, when they were like boys hunting with their bows, walking the bush without care. Just enjoying the day, not as PH and hunter, just as friends.

Lucas returns from the dream and tries to tell Gordon about the gun and why he didn't shoot the buff.

"Gordon, a mistake was made today, a rather serious one, and I'd like to talk about it."

Gordon knows what's coming. It's either the empty chambers in the gun, or standing to take the buff's charge. In any case, he's not ready to face his mistakes as the liquor is taking its affect. He would like to do this sober knowing how alcohol fuels emotion, and he's finally beginning to feel good again.

"Lucas," he replies, "if it's all the same to you, I'd rather do the hunter and PH thing tomorrow. We've got one last night, we both did well today, and everything turned out as I'd planned except for the swelling and the bleeding, which is only temporary. If you don't mind I'd just like to celebrate a dream come true."

"Can I just ask you one thing then, Gordon?"

Fearing the ugliness about to start, but knowing it has to start to get finished, Gordon looks Lucas in the eye and says, "Sure, Lucas, ask me anything."

"Why did you stand and take a buff charge with nothing more than a longbow? That was insane."

Relief sweeps Gordon until he's flushed with warmth and he replies, "First of all, good man, my bow is good and you've seen me take plenty of African game with it."

"I've seen you lose also, my friend, and you haven't taken anything like a buff before."

"You didn't see the first two shots until it was done. They were both good double-lung arrows. That buff was dead standing."

"More than a few hunters have been hurt by buffs they thought were dead, friend."

"I know, Lucas," Gordon starts again, "But when he turned to face me I knew the first two shots were good and I could just see the last shot. I saw it before it happened. I don't know how to explain it any different than that, but I could just see the shot coming."

"You're a lucky man you made that shot, if you hadn't, I'd still be picking up your pieces out there."

"Let's not talk about what might have happened. We've got a great story for our grandchildren. We have ourselves a great old Dagga Boy, and we have dozens of pictures. Let's just celebrate."

"You're a pain in a PH's rear."

Gordon smiles because he knows it's true. He knows the easiest thing a PH can do is take a rifle hunter into the field after plains game, get them half a dozen animals in the same number of days, and take them home early each day for drinks and listen to their stories. The PH will get a heavy tip at the end of that week and the hunter will go home swollen from the back slaps, the "good shots", and the thousands of photos of himself, his rifle, and his conquests. Gordon also knows the likely impossibilities of stalking with a hunter carrying a longbow. And he knows the rewards are fewer but they are far sweeter.

Gordon says, "I know, Lucas, I proved that today for sure, but isn't it great when we succeed?"

"What's great is just to have it done,"

"Indeed it is, great to have it done."

Lise calls them both for dinner and they spend the rest of the night telling their story, in the greatest detail, to the other guests in camp. By ten o'clock the camp generator shuts off and everyone's in their beds.

Gordon's still awake in his tent, almost afraid to go to sleep. His conscience just won't let go of the cartridges in his pack. He's also had too much to drink, and not being a regular drinker, knows that he won't sleep because the alcohol disturbs the peace that the mind usually holds during sleep, so now good sleep is probably not possible. He sits on the cot in his tent with the pack beside him and reaches into the inside pocket to pull out the shells. Running his fingers up and down the cold brass cartridges in the dark, he raises them to his nose to breathe the smells of lead and brass and then drops them onto the bed. He fishes out his headlamp, journal, and pencil and begins to write.

"Gordon, may I come in?" The zipper on the tent is pulled from the bottom up to open but no one enters. Startled, his swollen face begins to throb again with the pulsing of his heart. He slides everything on the bed into a pile. The brass shells make an unmistakable sound as they clink against each other. Gordon winces at the noise, and his stupidity. He sets the pack on top to conceal the shells and the notebook.

"Sure, Lise, come in." She turns to pick up something from the ground behind her, and walks through the tent flap with a serving tray. Gordon takes off his headlamp and hangs it from a tent pole supporting the roof so they will have a little light to share while she's in his tent. Lise sets the tray on the only chair in the tent. She sits at the foot of the little bed, actually a cot with a small mattress. She expects Gordon to sit with her, but he's reluctant.

"Sit, Gordon, it's okay."

Gordon sits at the other side of the bed with the pack between them.

"I brought you some hot tea, and some ice for your face."

"That was kind of you."

"Gordon, I wanted to talk to you about something."

"Sure, Lise. Anything."

"Gordon, you could have been killed today."

"Not really."

"Yes, really. If that buff wanted to, he could have charged you after the first arrow and taken you with him. When I heard you tell the story, it scared me to death, Gordon. I care about you Gordon."

"I care about you too, Lise. I would do anything for you...and Luc. The buff hunt was exactly what I had planned, no guns, just the Cape buffalo and me, intimately sharing a moment." She pours and he takes the tea from her. He sips it and puts the hot mug on his throbbing forehead.

"I know Lucas can be headstrong and wants to do everything his way, Gordon, but if you're going to keep hunting dangerous things you're going to figure out a way to listen to him so you don't get hurt."

"Lise, Luc is a fine PH. Some day I hope you and I can talk about today, but it's not time yet."

"I don't understand, Gordon."

"I'm not sure I do either, but some day maybe together, we can figure it all out. As far as continuing to hunt dangerous animals, Lise, I'm not sure I can. I'm not sure I'm coming back."

"What?" She raises her voice to an uncomfortable level. "What are you talking about? You're not coming back anymore? Gordon, why?"

"Lise, I said I'm not sure. There are things that are already done that may prevent it. I just don't know, Lise, it's a struggle to find the money every time I come. It gets harder and harder to leave every time I go. The only thing I do know is if I could see you again, I'd lose everything and start over. The only bad part is the best place in the world to start over is America, and you're not there."

"You would do that for me?"

"Lise, you're a married woman, and I've said too much. What we are doing here is innocent so far, but others won't think so, and I don't ever want people to think poorly of you. I'd feel much more comfortable if you left now. I'm already spinning out of control and I don't want to pull you into my tornado."

"But, Gordon — " But before she can get the words out, he interrupts her. "Please, Lise, Lucas needs you."

She leaves without a word, and walks home in the dark, wondering what just happened.

Unsettled

*L*ucas and Lise lie in bed. Lucas' sleep is disturbed by the missing cartridges.

He says to Lise, "If I could just find those two shells I might be able to figure out what happened."

"Did you tell him yet?"

"No, I tried but he didn't want to talk about it, I think he feels like crap, that buff really worked him over. Hopefully he's passed out and he gets some sleep tonight, and hopefully he doesn't have blood in his urine in the morning."

"We'll figure it out in the morning," Lise whispers. "We can search the truck and the camp for the bullets and you can talk to Gordon on the way to the airport. Everything will be good again. Now let's get some sleep."

She kisses Lucas and rolls over onto her left side away from him to sleep, signaling that the conversation has ended whether he's done or not, and she is going to sleep with or without him. Her day has been too long and she's putting an end to it. Lucas lies on his back, fingers interlocked behind his head, and stares into the dark, working out all of the possibilities and placing them in order of importance so he can start efficiently in the morning to find the shells and end his torment.

The minutes crawl by and his restlessness encourages him to get out of bed and write a thank-you note to Gordon. He turns on his headlamp and writes until Lise can't stand the light on any more. He closes the note card, slides it into its envelope, and places it under the knife that he wears every day so it has no chance of being forgotten. He decides to tell Gordon about the gun in the morning and then, like always, give him the note card at the airport. With his conscience lighter and sleep a better possibility, he gets back into bed and closes his eyes. Only momentarily does he have flashes of the open breech, and the empty chambers of the double rifle, and only a few times during the night does he wake in a full sprint to the buff. Otherwise, he does sleep some.

Thoughts of Dagga Boy

*T*he Askari works his way through the bush to the water hole where Dagga Boy met his demise. He doesn't like the darkness and he's never imagined possible the depth of loneliness that he feels now.

Herd animals just aren't good alone, he thinks. *I need to fill myself with water, and I need to find the herd.* He knows he's prone to a lion attack, so he moves in slow, stops, checks with every sense he has, and then he moves again. He misses the Dagga Boy, his lessons, and the way they worked together like all herd animals do. He works his way back to the place that Dagga Boy took the first two arrows. He smells the blood, and he stirs the ground with his hoof to release more of the blood smell into the air. Plains game animals don't like the smell of blood, unlike predators who love the smell and will do anything at all to find its source. The young bull only takes it in to remember. He wants desperately to remember Dagga Boy and everything, even the bad part, of their time together. He walks slowly to the place where Dagga Boy collided with the hunter and again he smells the bull's blood and also the blood of the bowhunter. Askari stands over the blood spit out by Gordon and breathes it deep into his sinuses because this too he wants to remember. The smell of Gordon's blood amid all of his sadness makes him strangely happy in a way unfamiliar to him. He thinks about the old Dagga Boy.

"You got him, Dagga Boy," he says filled with pride, "you took that hunter head on and you got him."

He scans the open area around the water carefully, and when he feels it's safe, heads in to drink.

Askari, the young bull hears the Dagga Boy.

"Dagga Boy, where are you?"

I'm gone, Askari, you know that, but you have to listen, says the old bull.

"But how?"

Just listen while we have this time. Take as much water as you can and listen to me. Askari, what happened was not your fault. That hunter was very good. He hunted in the old style, when they had to get very close to an animal to have any chance of killing it. Hunting that way gives them better skills and that hunter proved it today. You, Askari, knew that noise wasn't an impala. You knew you should see horns bouncing through the brush, but I insisted you were wrong, I let thirst cloud my judgment. I didn't trust you, the one sent to protect me. You knew, Askari, take that with you, you knew. When we stepped out of the bush and he grunted again, I knew he had you, he was closer than I've ever seen a man, the limbs of his bow were already bent to send the arrow, and you were dead, Askari.

"So why did you do it, Dagga Boy?"

Askari, it's for the good of the herd. I told you about sacrificing one bull for the good of the herd. This time it was me. I saved you to save the herd, you're my son, my genes, and to save you is to save our place in the herd. You're the future, Askari. You've learned a great amount in a short time and I'm very proud of you. Now it's your turn, Askari, to return to the herd and fight for your place in it. I want you to drink and drink all that you can, then go to the bush, wait and rest there. Before the sun rises I want you to come to the water again, take as much as you can, and then go find the herd. You'll have to fight when you get there to rejoin them. You'll fight for your females, and you'll fight to be the dominant herd bull. This is not where it ends, Askari, this is where it begins.

Askari, feeling overwhelmed by the charge he's been given, says, "Dagga Boy, I'm not sure that I can do all of that, I've never fought before."

Askari, that's why you were chosen to go with me, your whole life you've watched me defend and protect what's mine. You've listened to my stories and my lessons, and you have to know that it was for your benefit as much as mine because it's your duty to carry on in my place. I've shown you how to fight, and I've told you of my battles. All you have to do is remember, Askari, the rest will come. I'll give you two more lessons, Askari, don't you ever forget them. First, a coward dies a thousand deaths; a Dagga Boy dies but once. Second, as long as you remember me, Askari, I will live. Think of me, Askari, and I will hear you. You don't need to talk out loud to me. Just think.

The night becomes still and black except for the moonlight reflecting onto the muddy water and the ripples carrying across the pond from the young bull's tongue. Askari knows that his Dagga Boy is gone. He also knows that this means he is no longer an Askari. He will drink tonight and again in the morning like the Dagga Boy told him. Then he will find, rejoin, and eventually take control of the herd. He will fight and he will teach, just as the Dagga Boy did for him. He will carry the memory of his Dagga Boy, his father, forever.

Buff Hangover

*J*ordon wakes before the sun rises feeling as if he hasn't slept at all. He knows he did sleep some because he can't remember the whole night, which means for some of it, he was sleeping. His nose is glued to the pillow by dried blood. His congestion has caused him to breathe through his mouth all night, making his throat sore and his head pound. He tears his nostril from the pillow and walks to the sink for the welcome relief of the propane-heated water. He soaks his head until the blood softens and then he immerses each temple under the running faucet letting the hot water run down over his closed eyes until the throbbing somewhat subsides. He cups his hands and brings the water to his face, submerges his nostrils and snorts the warm water up his nose forcefully until he can feel the heat behind his eyeballs, and the gelatinous mixture of blood and mucus slide to the back of his throat. He swallows hard to force the mixture down instead of coughing it up and as it travels to his stomach it makes him shudder. He repeats the snorting of the hot water several times until he frees the rest of the mucus and blood from his sinuses. He blows and coughs and spits until everything is clear, except the sink. Then he tends to the cleaning. After washing himself as much as necessary to feel human again, he washes all of the grotesqueness out of the sink. He wrings the blood out of the washcloth so it won't be a mess for GoGo when she does the laundry, and drapes it on the edge of the sink to dry. He combs his hair with his fingers and searches the floor for something to put on. He pulls on a T-shirt, a fleece, and his khakis for traveling. He throws his old sneakers, some well-worn jeans, and a few shirts into a pile on the floor of his tent for the camp staff to fight over and so he can leave traveling lighter than he came.

He finds the .500-nitro cartridges on his bed as when he last saw them. He takes the letter that he wrote Lucas, neatly folds it into thirds, and wraps it over them. He fishes through his pack for a rubber band. He saves the heavy produce bands from the grocery store, the kind they bind heads of broccoli with and even the ones they use for binding lobster claws. They make great tools for a hunting pack and Gordon has found dozens of uses for them. He secures the note to the shells by looping the rubber band around it. He slips the shells and the note into his pocket and unzips his tent to go get coffee.

This really is one of the best parts of Africa for Gordon. He loves to be the first to the coffee and sit outside in the dark at the fire pit with the embers from the previous night still glowing under the ash. Alone, he thinks clearly, he looks at the stars and picks out one, then thinks how cool it is that someone half the world over may be looking at that exact same star at the same moment. The coffee feels good on his sore throat and he alternates the warm mug from eye to eye, then from temple to temple which seems to help relieve the pain and pressure from the swelling. He wonders how the day will begin when Lucas wakes, and then a distant impala breaks the silence. The barks resonate through the camp and Gordon chuckles, wondering if the impala ever sleep during the rut. He gets up and pitches some dry wood onto the coals and walks to the kitchen for a second cup of coffee. Turning the corner to the open door of the kitchen he sees Lucas standing at the coffee pot.

Lucas smiles and says, "I thought you were sleeping in, Gordy."

"I can't sleep, besides I don't want to waste my last day here. I'll sleep on the plane. I got the fire going, you want to sit with me and listen to the impalas drive themselves crazy?"

"Sure, I love being at this camp in the morning. When you sit at the fire pit with your coffee, watch the sun come up, and look at the view, it feels like you're sitting in the palm of God's hand. When you see how big this place is, it makes you realize just how small you are."

"I know, Lucas, it's one of the best things about hunting here. Sometimes I think about how many predators have come and gone, how many plains game animals have been taken and how everything is still the same. I realize I've had no effect at all except for one day with one old Dagga Boy. Other than that, this place goes on like I was never here."

"Gordon, we have to talk about yesterday."

"Sure, Lucas, what's wrong?"

Lucas stirs the coals and looks into the fire as he starts his admission, "Gordon, yesterday, when I didn't shoot, it was because I couldn't."

"I know you couldn't shoot, I was in your line of sight."

"Gordon, I'd made a hide and a gun rest out of a termite mound. I was seventy-five meters from that Dagga Boy when he walked out of the bush. I had my front sight on his spine when I saw you shoot."

Moses walks into the light of the fire and stands silently with a cup of hot tea.

"Hello, Moses, you want to sit with us?" Gordon offers.

"I here you cheated death yesterday, Gordon."

"Not to be contrary, Mo, but I lived life to its absolute fullest yesterday."

"You performed well under pressure, Gordon, how did Lucas do?"

The question strikes sharply and rings in the ears of both men like a blacksmith's hammer hitting an anvil. Lucas hides his discontent with the inquiry and Gordon makes clear his satisfaction with his friend and guide.

"Brilliant, simply brilliant. He had me in his sights the whole time, Mo, but didn't shoot, just like I asked."

"We don't like our clients getting hurt. There are liabilities to this happening in our camps." The unspoken message is clear.

Lucas begins to feel the dung that slides downhill and lands on the PH at the end of a hunt with a bad client. It's an-all-too familiar slumgullion of fecal matter that he's learned to traverse during his years in the field. Management is always correct and the clients are always correct, even when both of them are wrong. The good PH will just wade through it, shake clean on the other side, and start again with a new client as if nothing has happened.

Gordon responds to Moses' comment directly. "Moses, for a brief moment I was intimate with that buff and that is exactly how Lucas and I had planned it. The buff was close enough to kill me but I killed him. Lucas was close enough to keep me safe and even tried to draw the buff's charge but that old Dagga Boy and I had locked eyes and nothing could keep us from finishing the other. It was a good way for the buff to die and it was a good way for me to do it. I'll remember this hunt forever and I have Lucas to thank."

"There are no bullets in my speech, Mr. Gordon," Moses responds more formally, "I only wish to say what is true as openly as I can."

"There are no shields in my answers, Moses. The injuries I have are at my own hand, and I am very proud of them."

Seeing that he may have offended both of the men, Moses walks to kitchen for a refill of his tea and leaves them to finish their coffee. Lucas looks down at his feet, then at Gordon and continues his conversation.

"They were empty, Gordon. The chambers were empty. I pulled the first trigger, then the second, neither fired. That's when I ran at the buffs and you."

"Lucas, I asked you not to shoot." He lets the words hang in the air. "I didn't want your help, and things turned out good, so no hard feelings."

Lucas can't understand because he's always been sure of one thing, that Gordon and he are honest with each other, good or bad, they have always been honest. Now it seems that he's made some grave mistake assuming that Gordon has deceived him. Then the flood of insecurity returns and in a simple, single moment he finds himself reviewing the possibilities of the missing cartridges.

Excluding Gordon, Lucas sees in his mind's eye the trackers un-loading the rifle when they prepared the truck early that morning. He sees himself leaving the shells somewhere in camp and forget-ting to load it. He sees himself pulling the rifle from the truck when they found the buff tracks. One thing he knows for sure is that he didn't check it when he pulled it from the truck. But why should he have checked it? He knew it was loaded, he felt the cartridge wallet and felt the two missing sleeves. This is his lesson. This is the thing he'll remember every time he touches a gun again. This is something that he's imprinted in his mind by his own mistake and it weighs heavy on his psyche and will for the foreseeable future.

"I don't know what happened, Gordon, I don't know if the trackers unloaded the gun, I don't know if I forgot to load the gun. All I do know is that I don't know."

"Well," Gordon answers, "I know three things, Lucas. The first is that everything turned out good despite what you think. The second is, you've proven that you're human. And the third thing, Lucas, is that you're honest and that means more than anything."

"It's a bad habit of mine, honesty, it's something I just can't seem to quit," Lucas replies, feeling relieved at the ease at which Gordon accepted the mistake.

Gordon's stomach tightens at the words. He knows he's in the middle of a lie and that he could end it all right now if he could just be as clean as Lucas is. He finds himself strangely disappoint-ed that Lucas did admit to attempting to shoot his buff, even when he had asked him not to. Gordon, for some reason can't find the same strength in himself. He just can't do it and it pains him to realize this. He searches for the right thing to do or say. The morn-ing he is leaving may not be the best time to have a knockdown, drag-out fight with Lucas. What would Lise think? Maybe the let-ter is the best way to keep this between he and Lucas. Lucas didn't trust him, he didn't trust Lucas, and it turns out, they were both correct. Gordon's anxiety causes only a bad joke to surface.

"Lucas," he says, "I guess this can only mean one thing."

"What's that?"

Gordon pauses for the sake of creating drama. Then says, "No tip."

Lucas laughs because he knows he's got the upper hand in this game, "Well, friend, I wish you luck thumbing a ride to the airport. I hope you don't get your throat cut and your bags stolen."

Gordon laughs but thinks about the situation he's put himself in, how very close he is to thumbing a ride to the airport, and that meeting a small band of poachers or other miscreants may well result in a severed throat.

"Well, you got me, friend. Maybe Lise would give me a ride. She likes me."

"Over my dead body," Lucas protests and Gordon realizes by the tone he uses that he may be less than willing to continue the conversation because Lucas knows that Lise does like Gordon very much.

Gordon and Lise have always had a relationship of respect and trust. They both seem to understand each other on a level that Lucas just can't get to with Lise. Since Gordon's first trip to Africa years before, he and Lise have always been content to sit and talk in the afternoons. Lucas always makes himself busy, thinking that if he isn't, someone may think he's irresponsible in his duties as the head PH of the camp. There's a calm to that part of the day for Lise, and both she and Gordon realize the importance of calm, quiet, moments, the time to think, and the time to talk to someone whose opinions you trust. There's never been any indiscretion be-tween them. They've just shared these quiet times well.

Sometimes Lise wants more than what she has. She feels less close to her husband than she would like and Gordon under-stands this about her most of all. She wishes that she could talk to Lucas the way she does to Gordon and that he would listen the way Gordon listens. Gordon wishes there were something he could do, but circumstance prevents involvement. Most of all, he wants not to be the cause of more complications for her because he cares more for her needs than he does his own, so he just talks.

Lise's days go well for the most part. She's busy enough to oc-cupy a day's time easily with her daily routine during the hunting season. Lucas sees how well and how easily Gordon spends even brief amounts of time with Lise, and it makes him resentful.

The Last Hunt

*G*ordon stands and stretches and says to Lucas, "Well friend, there's only one thing left to do."

"What's that?"

"Let's go for a walk with our bows, see what we can find."

"Sure you feel ok?"

"I feel fine for someone who just got hit by a Cape buffalo. Besides, it's what we do, so let's go."

"Let me eat something, and I'll get my bow from the house."

"Now you're talking. I left mine in the truck. I'll meet you back here. We can walk if you're up to it, old man."

"Don't test me, Gordon, or I'll walk you to the gate and bid you farewell."

Lucas walks to the boma and gathers a plate full of food, eggs, toast, bacon, sausage, and sprinkles some shredded biltong on top of the whole thing. He pours more coffee and turns to sit when Lise says, "No fruit, Lucas? No vegetables last night either. The makings of a sluggish PH with impacted bowels."

"The coffee takes care of both of those problems, dear."

"I think eating something green besides gelatin desserts would do you some good, Lucas."

"Got to have some protein. I'm going for a walk with Gordon. You know what a walker he is. I'll burn the calories by the time we get back and you can make me eat whatever you want for lunch, dear."

"Good, I'll make some shakes and we can take them to the airport with us."

"You're going to the airport with Gordon and me?"

"Sure, I'd like to ride along. I thought it would be fun to go and see him off. We could spend some time together on the way home, maybe stop for dinner while we're out."

"Know what, Lise? I think I'd really like that."

Lise sees the softness that Lucas rarely shows, and to show her appreciation she puts her arms around his shoulders and kisses him on the cheek.

Gordon walks to the Rover, opens the passenger door and reaches in for the unstrung longbow. He slides it out and leans it against the truck bed, then leans back in for his quiver, glove, and armguard. He looks along the metal dash, then down at the glove box. Making sure the open truck door is blocking Lucas' view, he turns the latch. The door of the glove box drops and Gordon catches it in his left hand. He reaches into his pocket and pulls out the shells and the letter. He places them carefully between the folded road maps, empty envelopes, and other discarded papers, pens, pencils, and an old pair of leather work gloves so they won't make noise during the drive. He pushes the glove box door firmly until the latch snaps closed and it's secure with his confession inside. Looking back, he sees Lise and Lucas. Taken aback by the public display of affection, he feels good for both of them because he knows they both need it. He thinks, *She's trying, that's good. Maybe he'll get it,* then closes the truck door and walks back to the fire to finish his coffee. Lucas devours his breakfast as if he's angry at it.

The Guinea Shot

*G*ordon and Lucas walk the dirt road from camp into the bush with their bows and back quivers. Lucas shoots two hares and feels very proud of his bare-bow skills.

"What do you think, pal? I'm getting pretty good at this long-bow stuff."

"You actually do impress me sometimes, Luc, but give me a chance to catch up."

This is the part of bowhunting they both enjoy, no pressure, just the two of them walking. They've talked and become close during these last-day hunts. They look forward to the last day as much as anything else they do.

Gordon sees a flock of guinea fowl feeding, quartering toward them, ahead and says, "Stay here and be quiet."

"Not again," Lucas jokes.

Gordon puts his rubber blunt tipped arrow back into the quiver and pulls out one with a new, razor-sharp broadhead. He angles forward and gets to his belly, sliding twenty meters in and out of brush and finds a place where he lies on his right elbow between bushes. The guineas are angling through the brush, pecking and feeding and Gordon anticipates their arrival by nocking the arrow and bringing the string to his cheek. His left arm folds up toward his face along with the bow's handle. He holds the bow, arms bent, right elbow in the dirt and left at his ribcage and waits, straining just to hold still. The birds begin to feed through in front of him at ten yards. Some run past his line of sight, some walk, and some stand and feed right in front of him. First one, then two, then two more birds stand pecking at the ground. He curls his fingers to hold tight on the string, and then slowly pushes the bow forward to full draw with his left arm. Confident in his target he tells himself *nothing moves.* He relaxes his fingers, the string and the arrow slip free. The arrow sails through the first bird and buries into the one behind. The guineas burst into the air but the two sharing the arrow stay behind. The one closest to Gordon has no use of its wings as it's been impaled just above both. An abbreviated stroke is all it gets out of them. The second bird tries frantically to fly but is weighed down by the first so it runs and feeling the forward pull of the shaft the other follows. They run, heads full forward until a termite mound breaks their momentum. They choose separate sides of the column of clay putting an abrupt end to their escape. The momentum of the birds and the sudden stop of the shaft against the termite mound cause the far bird to spin off the broadhead. As the guinea rotates free, the initial wound expands into a gaping hole and just as the bird is liberated, it falls dead. The arrow whips back around the termite mound and it turns the close side bird at an angle as it runs. The shaft is held in the bird by the feather fletching and the broadhead drags in the dirt until it snags a bush and pulls the fletching and the rest of the shaft through the guinea. Now free, the bird takes to the air, but in its panic to escape, it flies head first into a thornbush and gets fatally tangled. It struggles frantically and the thorns imbed deep into its flesh, making escape impossible. The struggle only lasts seconds until the bird loses its will to survive and then lies dead, suspended in the branches. Gordon dusts himself off and walks back to Lucas with a grin that he gets when things go well. *Thank you Lord, for making it quick.* Gordon prays.

Lucas looks at him, smirks along with him and says,

"Brilliant, just simply brilliant. That was quite a show."

"Thanks, I thought it was too."

"Well my friend, you've done good this trip. Anything else you need before we head back?"

"Unless you can find me a kudu in the next half hour I'm all good."

"Next trip, Gordon, there's always the next trip. By the way, you're not still stuck on that, are you?"

"Honestly, Luc, it still haunts me."

Gordon thinks about the kudu he lost on their first hunt together. It was the first African animal he'd ever shot and it became his haunting and still is. He's rarely gone hunting anywhere without thinking about it, and although it's deeply internalized, it's never left him. It rises from the depths of his psyche, from under the ashes of all the other things that are dead to him, and drives into him a great-spiraled horn that eviscerates him. It's almost become some cruel African curse upon Gordon. He loves Africa dearly but the punishment he bears is that he'll never be given by Africa what he came for in the first place, a kudu.

Lucas gives Gordon time as he sees his drifting mind and then says,

"You've done a lot, friend, let that one go."

"Luc, I am so lucky just to be here. I'm so lucky just to have seen and done what I have here. I know there are so many hunters less fortunate than me, and I know I should be thankful and I am, Luc, I truly am. But that kudu mistake just eats at me and it just won't quit."

"You know, Gordon, all PHs have nightmares. Nightmares about something they did or something they didn't do at all. Follow a wounded buff or lion into some tall grass and take the charge for your hunter who wounded it in the first place. You think about the charge for days, sometimes weeks after. Then the next time you do it the previous one comes back into your mind and breaks your focus and you have to break free of it quick before you make a mistake and get somebody hurt. Your mind can process good and evil so fast when it's fueled by adrenaline and fear that you have to stop all of your thoughts and focus on only sights, sounds, and smells and act or react in fractions of seconds. Then you hear about another PH who got his pelvis crushed by a buff, or his face torn off and his neck snapped by a lion, and you think of your close call again. Gordon, if you don't let that stuff go, it'll eat at you until you aren't safe to be around. That kudu mistake was just that, a mistake, nothing was hurt but your pride. Besides, your intentions were good."

"Thanks, Luc, I knew you'd reel me back."

"Telling someone else what they should do is usually easier than keeping yourself squared away, but I've seen enough bad things happen to know what you did, Gordon, should've been forgiven long ago."

"You ready to head back, Luc?" Gordon says changing the subject. He realizes his kudu mistake is trivial to Lucas who squares off with dangerous game for a living, and he begins to feel foolish.

"Yep, we'd better get you to the airport before it's too late."

"I'd hate to miss the fifteen-hour flight."

"Funnest part of Africa, isn't it."

"It's not bad after a few glasses of wine and a sleeping pill. I put the headphones on and sleep like a baby."

"You never could handle your alcohol."

Gordon picks up the guineas, stuffs their heads from the bottom up underneath his belt until they protrude from the top. He tightens his belt a notch flattening out their necks and begins to walk with the birds' bodies bouncing off his butt. Lucas has never seen something so funny, yet strangely practical. He begins to do the same thing with the hare but realizes the size of the heads make the task cumbersome.

"Turn 'em around," Gordon says.

"What?" Lucas doesn't quite understand.

"Here, let me help the mighty rabbit hunter."

Gordon sets his bow down and picks up the hares. He takes one hind foot from each of the hares, and tucks them up under Luc's belt on opposite sides of a belt loop. He pulls a rubber band from his pack and loops it several times around each foot above the belt, securing them for the trip to camp.

"There you go, buddy," Gordon says, "let's walk."

The two walk with their quarry bouncing off their butts, laughing at each other and trading insults but feeling as fulfilled as when they killed the buff, in a much lighter, less serious way. They cover the few miles back to camp with the ease that a happy ending brings to the hearts and legs of hunters and makes the last walk out a pleasure instead of a chore. They get to the camp lawn and give the birds and hares to Daniel who's waiting nervously for them to return safely.

"What's up with Daniel?" Gordon asks.

"He worries like an old woman," Lucas says. "He's convinced I can't do anything without him. He also thinks he's the best tracker in Africa and we might lose game without him. He considers it his duty to help me whenever I'm in the field. Daniel's fiercely loyal to me. I pulled him out of a bad place when we were young and we've been close ever since."

"That's something you never told me before. I know you work well together but I never knew there was a back story. What happened?"

Lucas and Daniel

"We met while I was apprenticing under another Professional Hunter. I'd just finished PH school and was working up near Polokwane, learning all of the stuff you don't learn in books. Daniel's father was the lead tracker for my boss and Daniel would work around camp, you know. He'd clean the camp, stack firewood, help the cooks, keep the salt shed clean, and if he got all of his camp work done in time, he'd help us track for clients. They worked him like a dog but he took it all in stride. It's like you could just see in this kid some kind of inner peace because he knew he'd be rid of the whole lot of them as soon as he was able."

"Was it that bad?"

"His father used to tan his hide for any little mistake. We'd be on a track and he'd go off on the wrong one and his father would grab him by the collar and throttle him right there in front of us. He'd get on the right track before the rest of us, and his father would beat him at night for showing him up at work. Daniel was good at everything he did and that was the problem, his father was scared. His father knew that young Daniel might be the first man to take his job from him."

"You take the bite out of the pup, there's no bite left in the dog," Gordon responds.

"Yep, he was willing to ruin his son for the sake of himself, but it didn't work. Daniel just kept getting stronger, smarter, and better. With every whipping, he came to realize it was usually because he did something better than his father."

"So what did you do?"

"I felt so bad for him, but I could also see him growing into something great. You know, some people would react to that by becoming what their tormentor wants, which is nothing. Others, like Daniel, see that you can learn what you don't want to be by watching a bad example and working to be better. Daniel was fourteen, but he was already a fine man on the inside. I was young and green, too, but he showed me something that I keep to this day."

"It's amazing that more people don't see the value in examples. We can learn something from anyone if we keep our minds open and put our judgments about them away," Gordon offers becoming more absorbed by the story.

"The PH I worked for was no pleasure either, so Daniel and I had kind of a kinship. It made us want to help each other. He'd do extra work for my clients, really made me look good. In turn, I'd leave him books where his old man wouldn't find them. He'd study the spoor, the scat, and he learned all of the English names for all of the animals we hunted. I'd let him know in advance what a client was hunting and he'd study everything he could about it. I really started raking in some tips, and a lot of it was because of how well Daniel and I worked together. Clients would leave Daniel stuff like hunting knives, clothes, and boots and I'd have to ask them to give it to me to hold for him because I knew his dad would take it from him. One client gave him a cloth measuring tape with metric on one side and American standard measurements on the other. That little tape did more for our careers than anything."

"How's that?"

"Daniel had grown to learn about the human ego, and the measuring tape was one thing he could hide from his father so he kept it with him always. I gave him a pocket guide to the Rowland Ward and SCI record books measurements, and he darn near memorized it. He kept it tucked in the waistband in the back of his pants. Every time we hunted together he'd pull out that tape and start measuring the kills while I was still congratulating the client. He was so animated, so effusive, that he kept everyone feeling great. If the animal made book he'd say, "Record book, record book, good show, sir!" He'd stroke the horns and pick the face up from the dirt and clean it and then ceremoniously hand it over to the client. If it were short of the book he'd give the same performance, but say, "Good bull, good bull sir, very close to the record!" He really made them feel good about their animals, and still does. He was young then, and there's something contagious about a kid's excitement. It wasn't an act either; Daniel was genuinely excited for the kill. As far as he was concerned, the animal was a team effort and he considered himself an integral part."

"So what happened?"

"I saved all I could for three years, all of my tips, and most of my salary. I was single then, so my expenses were small. I asked my clients for letters of recommendation. I saved all of the stuff for Daniel, too, in a footlocker. Then I found a man who owned a good concession and was willing to take a chance on a young PH and an even younger tracker."

"What did his dad do?"

"Well, what could he do? I took Daniel on a walk one day and told him I was quitting. I told him I had a new job at a different camp and I wanted him to come with me to be my tracker. Daniel didn't even think about it and said, 'I already am your tracker.' It never occurred to me that he, more than I, already knew we were a team, and that if I left there was no question he was going with me. I told him we would leave in two weeks but not to tell anyone, and when it was time that he needed to pack his stuff in the footlocker in my room and we'd load the truck and go. His dad wouldn't have time for another beating because we'd be driving out the gate."

"Did it go badly?"

"Well, my plan was great on paper, but I didn't plan on how mad my boss would get when I gave him my resignation."

"What did he do?"

"I went from the golden boy to a bum in a breath. I was the most ungrateful, worthless, poor excuse for a PH that ever walked that concession. He didn't accept my resignation, and he didn't accept my two weeks' notice. He fired me right then and told me to get out before night. I was kind of panicked at first because this old guy was the kind who wouldn't think twice about taking a swing at you, and then there was Daniel and the logistics of his escape."

"How did you get the word to him?"

"I was really worried about finding him and getting him away from his father long enough to let him know what was going on. I searched all over camp for him and was figuring I'd have to get out and come back later for him or get word to him what had happened and make another plan. I looked everywhere and I was running out of time so I went to my room to pack. When I got there Daniel was leaving. It surprised the crap out of me."

He said, 'Mr. Lucas, I'm ready.'

"'What are you talking about, Daniel?' I asked him, I had no idea how he could have known."

"The cook heard the boss screaming at you, and sent one of the old women to listen. When she told him what was happening, he sent all of the help to look for me.'

"'They weren't supposed to know you were leaving with me, Daniel.' I told him. I was pretty hot at the whole situation and at the stress of being kicked out. Finding out Daniel had told other people our plan really disappointed me and I was seriously thinking about sacking the whole idea, driving away, and leaving it all in my rearview mirror."

"Daniel could tell I was really mad and he pleaded with me, 'I didn't tell, Mr. Lucas, I swear on the life of my mother I didn't tell. The others in camp know you're my PH and I'm your tracker. They know if you need help, I help, just like you help me.' I asked him, 'What are you doing here, Daniel?'"

"I put my belongings in your footlocker like you told me, Mr. Lucas. I'm ready, and no one knows."

Gordon interrupts, "So you're panicked and this kid's just steadfast to the plan."

"That's pretty much how it went, so I got all my stuff together and we loaded my truck and everyone thought it was just me leaving because Daniel's stuff was in my footlocker and everything was almost over when Daniel threw me another curve."

"Did he have second thoughts about leaving?"

"No, he was stuck on leaving."

"What did he do?"

"He had to tell his father goodbye. He couldn't leave without facing him. He said it would be disrespectful of him to leave without thanking his father."

"That's incredible," Gordon says.

"I know, Gordy, and I had to honor it. I couldn't make him leave before his business was finished. We waited for his father to get back from the bush that evening. Everyone in camp was told to go about his or her regular duties and ignore my leaving so there wasn't any big deal made over me. Most of the camp help just winked or nodded to me and the brave ones would give me a handshake. The other PHs in camp said their goodbyes privately, already knowing we would see each other again, nomads we are, you know. Then came Daniel's turn."

"I'll bet that was something," Gordon says waiting for the end of the story.

"I wanted to make Daniel feel good about going with me, so I took him over to my truck and had a talk with him. I told him about the things in the footlocker, that they belonged to him. I told him that the clients had left all of the gifts for him, and I told him I was very sorry for keeping them from him, but I didn't want his father to take them and now the whole trunk belonged to him. The clients gave these gifts to him because they recognized the value in his skills and his work. Then I gave him one month's pay in advance, told him I was glad to have him as my first employee, and told him I was very excited about our work together and our future."

"What did he do?"

"Daniel was stunned, first, and then he was very, very proud. He was proud that there were people who recognized his skills and his value. He was touched that people saw in him someone that was good. Then what I saw in Daniel was resolve, it swelled in him, you could see it build. This was a moment of confirmation for him, it made unmovable his decision to leave."

"His father rolled in on the back of the truck from the bush. His was the last truck back that evening, all of the guests were in camp and everyone was having starters and feeling good. Daniel's father saw us together and walked over to give him some crap about standing around in front of the guests while they were having sundowners.

"He was all business, that man, and all about image. He wore clean green coveralls, oiled boots, and a matching belt. He even oiled the sheath of his hunting knife to match. The man never smiled in camp and he always barked at Daniel and the others to make it clear he was their senior staffer. He was a big, mean, powerful man with a persistent bad attitude toward the rest of the staff, and he was quick to jump in where he wasn't actually needed. Daniel saw his dad and walked to him without a second thought."

"What were you thinking, Luc?"

"Well, I did start the diesel just in case, but to tell you the truth I was already past all of the drama, I just wanted to get the hell out of there and let my new boss know we'd be coming earlier than expected."

"So what happened?"

"So Daniel walks up to his father but before he can say anything his dad barks, 'What are you doing, Daniel? Get out of the boma.'

Then Daniel says, 'Father I need to talk to you.'

'Not now, I have clients I must attend to, go and I'll talk to you tonight.'

'Father, I'm leaving.'

'Good, get out of here, I'll talk to you later.'

'Father, I'm leaving you.'

'I said good, now go.'

'Father, I'm going to work for Lucas, we are leaving camp tonight for employment in Thabazimbi... I just wanted to say goodbye."

"The glue holding that man together began to melt, all of the rage and anger he had in him was becoming unfastened, and you could see hate pulsing the veins near his temples. Then a portly old German hunter with a fist full of biltong and a beer walked by and Daniel's father realized a catastrophic meltdown there wouldn't be in his best interest. He snatched Daniel by the arm, which drew more than a few stares from the guests, and marched him behind the kitchen."

'You are doing what?' his father asked.

'Father, I'm leaving. Lucas has taken a job in Thabazimbi and has hired me to be his tracker. I've received my first month's salary and all of the tips I earned from his clients here and I'm leaving tonight.'

'You thankless little son of a whore, I'll give you a hiding you'll not forget, ever. You're not a tracker, you're not a hunter, you're just a hide-scraping salt-shed boy and you don't even do that well.'

"The tension was pretty thick and the other PHs were moving toward the kitchen to buffer the situation. They wanted to give Daniel and his father space, but they also knew that their clients' best interest was a quiet, peaceful camp. Happy clients tip well and their money takes precedent over a family dispute. I just sat back and watched it all unfold, knowing that if he got too rough on Daniel, I'd bust his snotlocker. I had nothing left to lose, and I wasn't about to watch him berate and bully that kid again. I'd seen it too many times before, and I was sick of being good, Daniel and I, and ending up in a pile of dung for it. Then we'd simply leave.

"It was getting kind of loud so this guy, Bossie, one of the senior PHs in camp, shows himself around the corner of the building and the message he had was clear, shut up or take it somewhere else. Then Daniel did something I never thought I'd see."

"He didn't hit his old man, did he?"

"No, even better. He got right into his father's face with all the PHs and me watching. He took a breath, and he began to speak.

'Father, I am leaving, and I'm leaving today. There's nothing you or anybody else here will do to stop me. I have a job of my own that I earned myself. I've worked hard to learn the skills I need. I've studied English so I can speak and the clients can understand me, and I them. I've studied all of the animals in South Africa, how to hunt them, where to shoot them, and how to track them.

I can eviscerate them, cape them, and separate every part cleanly for food. I've done every job in camp and have learned to do them well. Now it is my time to go.'

"'I've taught you everything you know, you disrespectful little snake in the bush,' his father spit through clenched teeth.

"'You've taught me only how to take a beating, only that when I'm sleeping at night or when I'm alone at our home you'll whip any mistake I've made, no matter how small, out of me. You've taught me to be afraid of you every minute of every day since I was a small boy, but that time has now past. I know now, father, that I am a stronger, better man than you will ever be.'

"His father grabbed him by his collar but Bossie made a quick whistle and stared him into letting go.

"'Because I could take all of your punishment, wake up every day, try harder, study more, work more, and appreciate the chance I had to improve myself.'

"'You appreciate nothing." his father snapped back.

"'I appreciate everything, father, that is the point. I appreciate the animals that die for us. I appreciate the country in which we live. I appreciate the PHs who helped me learn so much. The cooks, the cleaning ladies, the rest of the staff, and the clients, I appreciate them all. They have all helped me to learn and I will never forget them. You, father, have little appreciation for anyone. You bully everyone in camp, even your own son. When I was young, I wanted nothing more than to be like you. As I grew, I realized that you were the worst kind of man to be. My sons will be raised differently, father, as I have had you, the best example of the worst father a boy could have. Be proud, though, father, the grandsons that you may never know will be fine men. They will grow to be strong, smart, hard-working, and honest and it won't be because they were beaten like dogs or mistreated like you've raised me. They will be raised to appreciate every opportunity, no matter how small, life offers them, and to always be prepared to take them. Now, father, my opportunity is here, and I am taking it.'"

"Then what happened?" Gordon asked.

"Nothing at all. All the PHs had gathered by that time and all had heard Daniel's speech. One was looking at the ground, trying not to laugh because Daniel's old man couldn't do anything about what was happening. One looked as if he'd just heard the coach's speech before a rugby match. Me, I was so proud of that kid, but I really did want to hit the road before the dung hit the fan. Then, I looked at Bossie."

"What did he do?"

"That big tough son of a gun had a tear rolling right down out of the corner of his eye. He looked at me and when our eyes met he nodded as if to say, 'it's time, take care of yourselves, get out while it's good.'"

"What did Daniel do?"

"He simply turned and walked to the truck and when he passed me he said, 'Lucas, I'm ready to go now', so we did."

The Long Drive to Johannesburg

The time had come to leave for the airport in Johannesburg and Gordon was becoming lost inside himself. Thinking about Daniel's story, the buff, and the mutual distrust he and Lucas had during the hunt.

The Rover was packed and except for handing out a few last gifts to the staff, Gordon was ready to leave and get this chapter of his life completed. He was beginning to feel good, very good, about killing the buff on his own though the sacrifice he forced may be a great one in the end. Lucas turns the key to let the glow plugs warm, and then eases it forward again until the diesel turns over and clatters to life expelling a small cloud of smoke. Lise walks up to the truck with three large drinks held to her mid section by her left arm. She hands one to Gordon and says, "Here you go, Gordon, a drink for the road trip."

"Thanks Lise, that's awfully nice of you," looking at the foamy, chunky, speckled drink, "What is it?"

"It's a peanut butter protein shake, it's good, trust me."

"Don't trust her," Lucas says over top of the diesel noise, "it's liver and whiz. She's trying to kill us with all of that good-for-you organic stuff."

"It is good for you," Lise continues, it's just peanut butter, yogurt, flaxseed oil, almond milk, honey, banana, and a handful of nuts."

Gordon takes a large swallow and finds it not just good but very good. He wonders why Lucas fights this stuff. All Lise wants is to help him be a little healthier and maybe even lose a little weight, too.

"Wow, Lise, that's really good, thank you."

"Pleasure, are we ready to go?"

"Well yes, I guess, are you coming too?"

"I thought I'd ride along and keep you guys company."

"That's great, you can ride up front with Lucas."

"Please no, Gordon, you're our client, you take the front."

"No way, Lise, I won't hear of it, you please ride up front with Lucas. Besides, I may catch a nap while we go."

"If you two are done with all of the politeness, I'd like to get on the road," Lucas says sarcastically.

Gordon and Lise look at each other and roll their eyes in unison and Gordon climbs into the back seat.

Gordon's glad to be on the road, though leaving Africa always gives him a visceral ache, like a magnetic pull he has to fight through to get to the airport. He thinks about the kudu again. The one he'd lost and the ones he never had a chance at after that. Then he thinks about Lise and that he might never have gotten that old Dagga Boy if she hadn't convinced him to let go of the kudu. As he watches her climb into the front seat, he realizes how good she is for him. He hopes he's brought something good to her life too. He thinks he is sure that he loves her, he's just not sure how, and he doesn't want to screw her life up by letting her know. Besides, he'll probably not be welcome to their concession, or their lives again.

Watching the people in the small towns as the Rover speeds by, he thinks about the simplicity and the honesty of the good people and the outward dishonesty of some amongst them. They all seem to be one union of good and bad, like a healthy body with tumors inside. They try to contain as much bad as they can by simply being good, living good, and raising their children to be good. They have no other way. It's sad that the good people are so passive and unprotected but they seem happy just by being happy. They live in the moment and for the day because it may be all that they have. Happiness can often times be just food, shelter, and God. If you can manage to live without the complications of modern life, you can live without the stresses they bring. But these people don't hunt. Hunting brings its own complications to a life. Gordon has made so many complications of his life.

Being a traveling hunter is becoming a rich man's pursuit, and Gordon realizes he may be nearing the end of his run. Thank God for the Dagga Boy, it may be his last big adventure. The money it takes to hunt dangerous game in Africa leaves the opportunity for only the wealthiest of nimrods, and that's not Gordon Bradford. He's had to save, to live simply, and to use the recompense from a sky miles credit card to afford the airfare. The deer hunting in America is still free, and he has turkey and black bear in his back yard, but that isn't Africa. It's not puff adders, mambas, leopards, and game that can hurt you, kill you if you make a mistake. There is still adventure in Africa, and adventure is something most men want their entire lives. As long as Gordon lives he will miss Africa, the animals, the tight spots he and Lucas have been in, the red wine by the fire at night, and the adventure that the next day always promises.

"Hey Gordy," Lucas says from the front, "How about filling out the paperwork for the buff and the taxidermist while we drive?"

"Not a problem, you gotta pen?"

"Look inside my notebook, Lise, hand that to him, the forms are in it."

Lise hands Gordon the old, stained, leather portfolio that she gave Lucas when they first met. She gave it to him to help him look more professional as a PH. She knew he performed well in the field, but she wanted him be as professional at camp and in the office too.

"There's no pen in here."

"Look in the glove box, Lise, find Gordy a pen."

Gordon sucks a breath and moves from Lucas' view in the rear view mirror because he knows the shock of what Lucas just said is unavoidably obvious on his face. He waits for the discovery of the shells and the letter and the explosive outburst that Lucas may have, and hopes he doesn't wreck the truck in the melee. Lise fishes through the glove box, dishing out stray papers and maps, and fondling the other things inside for their identification. Her fingertips find the shells with the note and rubber band and she curls the assembly into her palm before realizing exactly what it is. At the shock of what she's just found she too can't breathe. It causes her to squeeze hard the package in her hand, and her entire body becomes hard. Her mind rushes through the shells with what she knows is Gordon's note, the deception Gordon has committed upon her husband, Lucas' reaction to being deceived, and the whole world inside the Rover turning into pandemonium. She freezes for a moment straining to think clearly through the tumbling thoughts, then before her mind collapses she breathes and releases her grip on the shells letting them slide back into the bottom of the glove box. She shuts the door, sealing the secret until some later time when she and Lucas can work on the problem together.

"Let me look in my purse."

She fishes a pen from the small bag she carries and hands it to Gordon without saying anything to him.

"Thanks, Lise." Gordon says about the pen and the secret, not knowing if she actually found the cartridges or not but thinking that she must have.

She says nothing in return only turning her attention to her husband, "So where will we eat after we get rid of Gordon?" She says sharply, releasing some of her annoyance.

"You mean after we drop him at the airport, dear?" Lucas returns wondering where the comment came from.

"Yes, isn't that what I said?"

"I guess, Lise, maybe we should get something in Jo'burg before we head back."

"Okay, Luc, but no fast food, you're taking me someplace good."

"All right, Lise, no fast food."

Gordon sits in the back seat trying not to be noticed, filling out the paperwork as fast as possible, and keeping his mouth shut because now he's managed to alienate the one person in Africa he's always been close to.

Lise sits in the front seat looking out the window and, as she always does, tries to think of Gordon's side of the story. What possibly could have made Gordon steal the bullets from Lucas? What did Lucas do to cause the distrust from Gordon? Then she gets mad at herself for doubting her husband and thinking that he may have, even if indirectly, caused Gordon to betray him. She gets mad at the situation that the three of them are in because, usually, wrong is wrong, but sometimes wrong is just one person's perspective and she knows and trusts Gordon and his deep, thoughtful perspective on most things. She's often thought how nice it would have been to marry a man like Gordon, someone who will sit and talk, and listen, and give honest opinions and emotions easily without any fear or hesitation. Then she gets mad for thinking that Gordon may be the good guy and Lucas may have caused this. She spins in her own thoughts and before she explodes she exhales, and then she begins to cry just a little.

"What's wrong, Lise?"

"Nothing, Lucas, I just get off the farm and it reminds me how lucky we are." She tells the truth but hides a lie behind it.

Gordon finishes filing out the papers, closes the book, and hands it to Lucas who drops it on the seat between him and Lise.

"Lise, you get off the farm all of the time, you don't cry every time you leave, do you?"

"No Lucas, I don't cry every time I leave."

Lucas gets an uneasy feeling about Lise and Gordon and asks, "Are you crying because Gordon's leaving?"

"No, Lucas, actually I'm quite glad he's leaving."

Surprised by the strangeness of the answer he begins to succumb to jealousy, "What on earth do you mean by that Lise?"

"I just mean I'll be glad to spend some time alone, with you, Lucas."

"Are you sure that's what you want? I could leave you two alone and thumb it home."

Gordon listens to the volley and can't forgive himself for what he's causing, the position he's put Lise in, and the accusation Lucas is trying to force upon her.

"Luc!" Gordon says sharply.

"What!"

"Lise is upset because she found your shells in the glove box."

"What?"

"She found the shells in the glove box when she was looking for a pen. She didn't know what to do because she didn't want you and me fighting at a hundred kilometers an hour down the highway. I put the shells there this morning before we left. I took them from your gun yesterday while I was getting the face paint from my pack because I knew you'd betray me. I knew you'd shoot my buff, so I betrayed you first."

"What are you talking about, Gordon? Betray you? I've never betrayed you. You took my shells, left me defenseless, I could have been killed, and then you lied about it."

"Lucas, you know you'd planned to shoot that buff, regardless if I needed your help or not. You were going to end it your way, the safe way. I asked you not to shoot my buff but you didn't listen."

"I was trying to save you from getting stomped into the earth!"

"You were trying to end it before it even began, safe, and sterile. As long as Lucas gets the buff on the ground and the client gets the photos, the truth of how it got done doesn't really matter."

"What do you know about the truth, Gordon?"

"I know I just beat you at your own game, and that's the only reason you have to be mad at me."

The conversation gets louder as it progresses until the two men are shouting at each other and Lise, somersaulting with emotion, pulls the letter from the glove box and begins to read it loudly. She grabs a hold of Lucas's hand and squeezes it hard to shut him up and then, when the two men are quiet, she starts at the beginning again.

Lucas,

Since our first safari together we have been like brothers and I hope that will never end. The mistake was not yours, Lucas, it was mine and it was no mistake at all. Lucas, I did the wrong thing because I knew you would do what you thought was the right thing. I knew you would shoot my buff, and I know you tried to shoot my buff. The missing shells, Lucas, I did that. I want you to know that I didn't plan to do what I did. I reached over the seat of your truck to get my face paint and I saw your rifle, packed tight between all of the lunch coolers, the extra jackets, and the spare boots. I was drawn to it, I knew it was wrong, but I did it, Lucas. I opened the breech, removed the cartridges, and stuffed them (no...I hid them) in my pack.

I know you think I must have prosthetic testicles for telling you this way, and I'm disappointed in myself too, but I wanted our time together not to end badly.

Lise begins to cry again because she realizes Gordon's side of the story may have some merit, a little anyway, or at least she knows Gordon and her husband well enough to understand what he's trying to say.

She continues,

Lucas, I know you don't understand, but I just couldn't feel good about a Cape buffalo that was killed by your rifle. For the rest of my life, I would look at that old buff knowing that you killed him for me. I'd rather not have it at all. I know it's your duty to keep me from doing stupid things and you've pulled me out of tight spots before. I can't thank you enough, but I just can't live with you shooting animals for me, and had I left it up to you, you would have done it. You would have shot that buff. You must understand that for me. Lucas, Africa has infected me, and I'm frightened of this thing that I've become. I've never lied to you or cheated you or taken advantage of your kindness. I've always wanted, more than anything, just to be treated as family and not as a client. That day when I stole your cartridges, I stole your trust. When you said I could take the lead I knew you would cover me, but I didn't want that. I wanted the buff my way. That's why I sent you north and I went south. That's why I told you to stay high enough out of their wind and to take cover to shoot from. Lucas, I didn't want you there, I didn't want you to get hurt.

She stops to sob, and begins to understand Gordon's intentions were not all bad. Then she collects herself and reads on.

I shot that buff good, two times, double-lunged him and I was ready just to sink into the bush and disappear until his lungs were filled and he drowned in his own blood. You changed the plan. First, you tried to shoot my buff when I asked you not to. Second, you were so dead-set on saving my ass, you ran screaming into two Cape buffalos. That, I think, was more insane than what I did, and it changed the whole game. If you, unarmed and outweighed (slightly), had been killed by those buffs I'd have never been able to live with myself, so I stood to take the charge. That big buff knew you were coming but he also knew that I was the one who killed him and he, above all, wanted to kill me first. As long as he was coming to me and not you I didn't care what happened. I knew he didn't have much left in him, I knew I had that last shot, and I knew the business we had left was between me and him alone. The irony here is that if you had just watched and trusted me, instead of trying to shoot the buff, it would have all ended quietly. There wasn't any reason to trust me though, but you didn't know that then. I didn't trust you, and I was right also. Sabotage, camouflage, and acts of treachery all come apart in a very ugly way sometimes and cause irreparable harm to people. We both mandated our will upon each other; we lost faith, for some reason, in each other. That may be the end of us and it may not, we'll see.

In the end, it did work out well. We got the buff and we didn't get killed doing it. I understand that I've lost your trust and that I may never regain it. I hope you understand I did it because I didn't trust you and I turned out to be right too. We've been like brothers since that first safari together. If we never see each other again it's my fault. I hope you think this through before you hunt me down and kill me and I hope, some day, you'll forgive me.

All my best, no matter what you decide, Gordon

Lise continues to cry and holds onto Lucas' hand for support, and to remind him support is what she needs and not for him to go ballistic and make the whole thing worse than it is, if that's even possible. Lucas drives steady on, pressure building to explosive levels inside him, but the squeeze of Lise's hand keeps the outward ugliness in, and he fights to be what Lise needs instead of what he wants to be. He imagines crushing Gordon's already bruised face with his fist as they drop him at the curb of the airport, tossing his bags out like garbage, and then spitting on him as he gets back in the truck to leave. Lise wouldn't care for this behavior, though. It's fine in the bush when a hiding needs to be handed out, but in public, especially in the city, discipline must be handled differently.

He searches to understand Gordon's side. To try to calm himself, he really tries to think like Lise thinks, to see with perspective like she does, but he can't get past the wrong that was done to him by his friend. Gordon's glad it's finally out. He feels free of the angst of holding a lie and he's glad, whatever the outcome, to have admitted it to Lucas. Now just the fight has to be completed and whatever the outcome, it will be in the past, and the past can never be changed so you don't worry about it.

"Lucas," Gordon tries.

"Shut up!"

"Lucas, listen."

"Shut up before I kick you out!"

"Lucas, you and I aren't far apart, we both deceived each other, I just did it to you first, that's why you're furious!"

"If you don't shut up, I'll throw you out!"

The shouting booms in Lise's ears and she trembles with anxiety and fear because she knows that both men are wrong and both men are right, but that Gordon committed a sin in the mind of all hunters. She does understand his motivation now, and sees Lucas from a different perspective. She knows he can be indifferent to her opinions but she thought that burden was just hers to bear. Now she knows he treats everyone the same and it saddens her to think of her husband that way. She reaches into the old leather portfolio and pulls out Lucas' thank you note. She tears the envelope open and screams above them both, *"Shut uuuup!"*

Both men break from the yelling and listen because they know they're probably hurting her most of all and they can see the stress she's under. She holds up the note card and reads,

GORDON,

WELL, MY FRIEND, YOU DID IT. CONGRATULATIONS! I SAY YOU DID IT BECAUSE I DIDN'T HAVE ANYTHING TO DO WITH IT. THE MISTAKE WITH THE GUN WAS MY OWN. TRYING TO SHOOT YOUR BUFF WHEN YOU ASKED ME NOT TO SHOWED MY LACK OF TRUST IN YOU. I PLANNED TO SHOOT THE BUFF. I'VE BEEN DOING THIS SO LONG THAT I'M NOT SURE ANYMORE WHERE THE LINE IS BETWEEN SAFETY AND TRUST. FOR THE MOST PART, I JUST MAKE THE SITUATION AS SAFE AS POSSIBLE, BUT MAYBE

I'VE FORGOTTEN WHAT'S IMPORTANT TO MY CLIENTS. FOR MOST HUNTERS THESE DAYS, BRINGING HOME A TROPHY IS THE MOST IMPORTANT THING NO MATTER HOW IT'S DONE. I FIND MYSELF IN SITUATIONS WHERE I HAVE TO FINISH AN ANIMAL FOR A HUNTER WHO FREEZES AFTER THE FIRST SHOT (OR SOMETIMES BEFORE).

I LOVE MY WORK LIKE NO OTHER PH BUT I'VE HAD TO DO A LOT OF UGLY THINGS FOR CLIENTS. I THINK THAT I'VE SEEN SO MANY MISTAKES THAT I TRY, NOW, TO PREVENT THEM BEFORE THEY HAPPEN. THEN COMES ALONG A HUNTER LIKE YOU, SERIOUS, PREPARED, INDEPENDENT, AND SOMEONE WHO KNOWS THAT THE HUNT IS MORE IMPORTANT THAN THE TROPHY. THAT'S NOT TYPICAL THESE DAYS; IT'S HARD TO TAKE A BACK SEAT TO A HUNTER, AND UNDERSTAND THAT HE WANTS, ABOVE ALL, TO HUNT FOR HIMSELF AND TO KILL FOR HIMSELF.

I PLANNED FROM THE BEGINNING TO KILL THAT BUFF SO YOU WOULDN'T GET HURT, EVEN WHEN YOU ASKED ME NOT TO. I DIDN'T TRUST YOU AND AS IT TURNS OUT MAYBE I SHOULD HAVE. IF YOU DON'T HUNT WITH ME AGAIN, THAT'S MY FAULT, AND I UNDERSTAND, BUT WE'VE BEEN MORE THAN CLIENT AND PH, WE HAVE

GROWN TO BE LIKE FAMILY AND I HOPE THAT DOESN'T CHANGE.

GOD BLESS,
LUCAS

Lucas realizes the admission in the letter. He's mad at Lise for reading it out loud and exposing his own sins to the light. For a moment he sits paralyzed by his own words as they echo through his mind. Silently the three drive to the airport, digesting the crimes committed by them and against them. They weigh out which is the worst and who should feel the need to apologize and if the other should accept or stay angry forever or at least until the pain of the betrayal is gone. Other than the sound of the tires on the highway there is nothing. The three of them sit in a bitter numbness, hoping it will end soon.

The Reckoning

The young bull, full of water, walks double time to find the herd. The reckoning in his life comes when he realizes it is his herd, Dagga Boy told him so, and in time, it will be. He misses his herd. He works to keep thoughts of them in his mind to mask the desperate loneliness. He imagines the females who one day will be his, the young there are now, and the young he will make in the future. He thinks about the time he'll have as the herd bull and his own time as a Dagga Boy. He remembers the bulls in the herd that will be waiting for him when he finds his way back. One by one he sees them and envisions the fight they have for him. One by one he plans a battle strategy for each bull his senior. He notes their strengths, their weaknesses, and ways to exploit them with his lessons. The bulls that were not Askaris don't have the lessons of a Dagga Boy, especially his Dagga Boy. Then he remembers that the Dagga Boy never taught him to fight and his heart becomes heavy again, but he walks on because he does remember the fate of a coward.

At first his eye catches just the wave of a black tail, then the haunches of a few young stragglers. He walks faster and as he does the images he sees become larger until the herd is standing in front of him in full and life sized.

"Look who's back," says the new lead bull. "Our own Askari, and I see that he's failed."

Askari hears the bull and is equally offended by what is said and who said it, the bull that took Dagga Boy's place in the herd.

"All Askaris fail, but you wouldn't know that because you were never chosen to be one. You've fought your way to the top of the herd without learning the lessons of leading a herd."

"And you think you can better me?"

"I think you will prove that for yourself, and I think the herd will soon see."

At this the bull lunges at Askari and strikes him with a mighty blow to the bosses that leaves his head ringing. Stunned at the power of the first blow, Askari doesn't brace for the second and it comes with more force and bad intent. It buckles his legs and he falls to the ground thinking the third may kill him.

Askari, get up.

Dagga Boy?

Get up, Askari, take this standing, DON'T LIE DOWN.

At this the Askari finds his feet. No longer does he question how Dagga Boy talks to him, he just accepts that he is there when Askari needs him and maybe that is a Dagga Boy's final duty. The large bull circles in for another blow.

Focus, Askari, you can't take him head on, he's too big. Focus on your timing. Your legs are young and fast. Use them to your advantage. Stand square with him, charge into him as he does you, but just before your bosses meet step to the side. Let him drive by you, not through you, son.

Askari does as he's told and finds the blows of the big bull are not as bad and his legs are getting slower with each pass.

Now, son, hit him with everything you have. Even if he still has more, you have more will.

Askari takes the bull square to the bosses and gives him his all. He strikes hard, then circles, strikes again, circles, and then strikes a third time. The older bull slows with the duration of the fight. He has the power but not the wind of the Askari.

Now, Askari, find his ribs. When he strikes, roll off him and as he passes you. Push as hard as you can into his ribs.

The Askari does as he is told and feels pleasure in hammering the side meat and movable ribs. The old bull bears the damage from the young bull but tires at the thought of taking much more, and then the final assault comes.

Now hook him, Askari, use your horns, get under his head as he passes and roll your horn into any flesh you can.

On the first pass the big bull feels the sting of the horn raking down his side skin. The second strike catches the bull across the shoulder. At the third the older bull intends to end the fight and strikes Askari so hard that it knocks the phlegm from his sinuses. The blow almost causes Askari to black out but he maintains consciousness until adrenaline rushes to his head and neck. He pushes hard and turns his horn into the big bull just under his jaw. The Askari's horn pulls at the loose skin until it is taut and then tears to the neck. The older bull has had many injuries, but never a tear to his flesh. As they circle for yet another charge, Askari is dizzy from the strikes to the head and cannot fully focus his eyes. The big bull feels the burn of the laceration, the blood that flows from it, and the bruised side meat. He realizes someone better than himself has taught this young bull to fight. They stare each other down. Askari no longer cares what's going to happen. He's punch drunk and all he knows is he is still on his feet and that means he hasn't lost or died. The big bull begins to doubt himself, the worst thing that can happen to anything that lives. He fears if he takes more damage from the young Askari he'll be looked poorly upon by the herd and be vulnerable to further attacks from the older bulls, then lose his place as herd leader.

As Askari's head clears he knows he is a herd bull and with a few more years of growth he will lead the herd. He proved it to himself today by taking on the largest bull, and he proved it to the herd.

The big bull stares through Askari. After gathering his breath he says, "This is over. You can stay, Askari, but keep away from the cows."

Askari says nothing, just walks into the herd and thinks, *the cows, I hope that's the next lesson.*

The Airport

The Rover pulls up to the curb at the departure gates. Lucas says nothing at all, just sits behind the wheel. Gordon gets out and swings his back pack onto one shoulder, pulls the old, worn, green canvas duffle from the back of the truck and hauls it up onto the other shoulder. He grabs his bow case and checks to see if he's forgotten anything. He turns to leave without saying a word, knowing that Lucas has no intention of saying goodbye or anything at all. He turns back to see Lise, her swollen eyes, and the makeup that she very rarely wears, smudged. He looks through all of it to see her and he thinks he most likely is looking at her for the last time so he makes the moment last. He mouths "sorry" to her, and turns to walk away.

She jumps out of the truck and hugs him. Sobbing again she doesn't have enough breath to make words, so Gordon says to her, "I love you, Lise." A flood of emotion roils her already fragile mind and body. She freezes stiff because she doesn't know exactly how he means what he just said. She doesn't know what to say or how to act until he clarifies his intentions. She loves him too, she always has but she's not sure exactly how, so she's frozen, afraid to stay, and afraid to go back to Lucas until she knows what Gordon means. Then Gordon simply says, "I love him, too," to let her off of the hook. He turns and walks away not wanting to interfere in their lives ever again.

Lise climbs into the truck an emotional wreck. Lucas just stares ahead without saying a word, checks his side mirror, and pulls into traffic. Lise looks back for Gordon in her side mirror but he's gone. Lucas gathers his thoughts, pulls a breath in and says, "Where would you like to eat?"

"What?" Lise exclaims.

"Where would you like to eat?"

"Son of a dog, Luc, you just let one of your best friends walk out of your life and didn't even try to talk to him, now you want to eat?"

Lucas pulls back over to the curb to accentuate the point he's making.

"Lise, he deceived me, he's gone now, back to America to go on with his life, and I'm going on, too. Where would you like to eat?"

"I can't leave this like nothing just happened, Lucas, I can't just internalize it all and go on, I just can't."

"What did he say to you Lise?"

"He told me he loved me." Saying this to get some sort of emotion, anything at all, from her husband, but this too, he swallows.

Calmly and directly Lucas asks, "Do you love him?"

"Of course I do, he's been a part of our lives for years."

"Did you tell him?"

"No, I didn't say anything at all, I was terrified by the whole thing. But I didn't want him to leave thinking we hated him, so I had to hug him like I always do, but this time may have been the last time. We may have just seen Gordon for the last time Lucas, and that hurts me. Don't you understand Lucas, I can't discard people as easily as you can."

Jealous, Lucas probes for more the way men always do when they're mad and they want a reason to get even angrier.

"What else did he say?"

"Nothing."

"He said something else, Lise, what was it?"

"It's not important, Lucas."

"What the hell did he say to you, Lise?"

"He said he loves you too, OKAY! He said he loves you, too. But it's not important because you don't listen. All you know is that you were deceived. Gordon did the wrong thing and you're irate because he committed some kind of offense against your manhood. What you're not considering, what hasn't even entered your thick, hard skull is that you contributed to the problem."

"What did I do?"

"YOU JUST DON'T LISTEN, Lucas. When someone tells you they want to do something on their own, that's what they want. They want to do it alone, especially hunters, and for sure, Gordon. No one except some of the drunkards that come here want to have an animal killed for them. No one wants you to kill a trophy for them, no one. Gordon has a whole process, a ritual. He's on his own path like a Muslim to Mecca. That's how serious he is about the killing. If he makes the decision to take the life of an animal, he does not want that to be an easy endeavor. He builds his own bows so that he has an intimate relationship with the weapon he uses. He chooses the weapon he uses so that he has to get within intimate distance of the animal he takes. It's a very personal thing. It's not ego, it's lack of ego. He has put himself willingly into a position where he has to work harder, focus more, and be more aware just to put himself into a position of having a chance at an animal. Even then, a chance is all he asks for, just a chance, nothing more, an opportunity to take an animal with all of the fairness he can give it. And then you admit to trying to swindle him out of that!"

"Lise, he took the shells from my rifle, I can't forgive that. Nothing is more offensive."

"Luc," she pauses to collect a calming breath. "What aren't you getting here? You premeditated a plan to shoot his buff too, Lucas. If you'd shot that buff, Gordon would have been destroyed. He'd rather take a shot and lose the buff than have you shoot it for him, any HUNTER would and no, Lucas, I DO NOT WANT ANYTHING TO EAT."

Lucas has no answer, only stares straight ahead, amazed that this, somehow, has become his indiscretion.

Gordon Says Goodbye

ordon sits at the airport bar, swollen face and all, drinking a cold beer and rolling the bottle across his aching forehead. Most of the other patrons glance, and he can see by their gestures that they think Africa's kicked his teeth in, and it has. Gordon just smiles back because it's better to fight and get your teeth kicked in than not to fight. After a fight is over and the pain is at a tolerable level, it's a great feeling to remember that you fought, especially for something good. The mud, clay, and sand of Africa are inside of him now, and he has left his blood and sweat in the African soil too. He thinks about his onlookers at the bar, *Bet they don't have a Dagga Boy, and even if they do they didn't get theirs like I got mine.*

As far as Lise and Lucas go, he's pretty much over them too. At least he's trying to be. He's never been really sure how he loves Lise, or she him, and it's just never been a good option to find out. She will always be in his heart, but he can't make a decision that she owns. For the rest of his life, whether she's with him or not, Gordon will love her, and he can live with that, because it happens to people all of the time.

He still considers Lucas to be a fine man even though he intended to shoot the Dagga Boy when Gordon asked him not to. Good people can have differing perspectives and still respect each other. He orders another beer and decides the best thing he can do is to leave them both alone to work their problems out. He doesn't want to cause any more for either of them. If she leaves, she'll call. If she doesn't, she won't. Either way he doesn't want to be a source of aggravation or a tool that they can use against each other. In the back of his mind he does think how good they could be, if they had the chance. He smiles as the people in the bar see his inward thoughts come to the surface like emotions often do.

An old Dutchman sitting next to him asks, "Rugby match?" Gordon smirks and thinks, *Sure, halfwit, I'm a forty-three year old American here playing rugby.* He answers, "Yep." That's all he says, but he remembers the hit the Dagga Boy laid on him and considers it the truth. Pulling into himself again he thinks about all he's done in Africa, and all it's done for him. The story of Lucas, Lise, him, and the Dagga Boy kind of sums up his feelings about Africa and why it's held him captivated for so many years. Africa holds beauty, strength, adventure, tragedy, ecstasy, and danger all together in its hands. Sometimes it cradles you and you're content to stay forever. Sometimes it claps its hands together, crushing you like a mosquito, so insignificant that no one knows you ever existed. Gordon's been three times in as many years, now maybe, one time too often. Chuckling softly he finishes the last swallow from the bottle, picks up his backpack, and as he walks to the gate he thinks, *next year...maybe I'll just hunt at home.*

An Old Friend

*A*s he boards the plane he notices an old friend and it makes his heart a little lighter. He smiles as their eyes meet from the opposite ends of the economy section. The pain of smiling reminds him what shape his face is in. She smiles back and grins at the bruising and swelling, and she winks her approval for the adventure that must have caused them.

He's getting his fill of Africa, she thinks with pleasure because, what little she knows about him, she knows as good.

Probably spoke out to the wrong person, looks like he received quite the hiding.

Gordon smiles because he knows what she is thinking and says to himself, *If you only knew.*

He lifts the duffle into the overhead and sits in the window seat praying no one will sit next to him. A few minutes later a fat man in a business suit sits next to him, his girth alone forcing Gordon's arm off of the armrest. They smile but Gordon makes no great attempt to start a conversation because he doesn't really want to relive the buff story or think about Lise at the moment because that's beginning to hurt a little knowing he'll think about her the rest of his life but never see her again. The businessman opens his laptop and begins to write like he has a deadline. Gordon just stares out the window hoping for the plane to get off of the ground and everyone to go to sleep so he can too. Eventually it taxis to the runway and takes off.

"Hello, my friend," a familiar voice comes from the aisle," can I get you anything?"

Gordon smiles and he looks to see the friendly flight attendant from his first trip to Africa. She reaches out her hand and he takes it into his,

"You were my first impression of Africa."

"I hope I represented it well."

"I'm still coming back."

"You're so kind to say so."

"Pleasure."

"Do you remember what I ordered on the first flight?"

"Two reds and a water, then you drink them all and fall asleep."

"Pinotage please."

"Can I get you some ice for your face?"

"It's not that bad."

"Still defending women from the drunks, I see."

"I got into a fight with a Cape buffalo. I won but he got a good lick in on me before it all ended."

The businessman stops typing, looks at Gordon over his reading glasses, and makes himself available to hear the buff story.

"Looks like he made you remember him," says the flight attendant.

"I'll remember him, I'll always remember him, like I'll remember you."

"I'll be right back with your drinks."

"Thank you, ma'am."

The drinks come. Gordon starts on the first glass of wine and stares out of the window. The engine noise, the crying kids, and the multi-cultural exchanges throughout the plane make Gordon withdraw into himself. He shuts down all of the input and tries to remember all of the Africa he has had and all of the Africa he has lost. The sounds blend into one as the wine, and the previous beers take their effect.

A woman speaking Afrikaans interrupts the man sitting next to Gordon. It's a voice he knows but can't place in that language, and he's losing tolerance for the noise and tries to shut her out, too.

"Verskoon, my sir." [Excuse me sir]

The man looks at her above the rims and says nothing to the interruption.

"Sou jy dit verander sitplekke met my sodat ek kan gaan sit met my man?" [Would you mind changing seats with me so I can sit with my husband?]

He looks at Gordon, head on the window and eyes closed, folds the laptop closed and stands. She directs him to her seat toward the rear of the plane. She sits and Gordon realizes what he thought he heard is what he knew he heard, but couldn't let himself think it because it would be too painful if it weren't true.

"Lise."

She lifts the armrest between them. She pulls Gordon's arm over her head and around her shoulders, puts her head against his neck, her legs over top of his legs until she can't get any closer to him. All she wants is to be held. As sleep overcomes Gordon, he smiles, completely content, and Lise closes her eyes to feel the moment, to bind it to her memory.

"Lise...how?"

"Merry Christmas, Gordon," is all she says and he has no idea what she's talking about but he sees her eyes closed, her smile, and he knows her heart and his are the same.

The flight attendant covers them both with a blanket. In Afrikaans Lise sleepily says, "thank you" at the same time Gordon says it in English. The flight attendant looks at the bruised and bloodied American who she knows is a good man, the pretty African woman with the tearstained cheeks, and knows their story, whatever it is, is something special. She wipes a single tear from the inside corner of her eye with her ring finger trying not to smear her makeup. She pauses to look at them, knowing they are of one heart and says simply,

"Pleasure."

I Will Tell Her

A s the stress of a taxing day brings sleep he closes his eyes. *I have to tell her,* he thinks, *She's been constant in my thoughts, and I have to tell her. I'll talk when she needs me to talk and I'll listen without talking. We can go on walks when I'm not working and we can find new things together. We can hold hands and sit outside in the evenings and drink coffee. We can start a new life together when we get home. When we get home, I will tell her.*

Lulled by the engine noise his head leans forward and to one side, against the window. It hangs resting. He's away from his family and friends. When he is he always worries. He's away from his home. But he has Lise and he realizes now that she is all he has ever needed.

He thinks about the way their lives will change. He'll have to change his life for her, and he will, when they get home, and this makes him happy.

A tapping noise on the window wakes him.

"Sir."

"Yes?"

"You can't park here, sir."

"Why?"

"This is the departure lane, Sir."

"But my wife, she's inside."

"Sir, you must leave."

"But, officer, she's not back yet."

"You've been here an hour, Sir. It's time, you have to go."

Thank you for reading <u>The Sound of the String.</u>

Please visit me at http://www.thesoundofthestring.com for the online Afterword.

Glossary of Terms

ANC – African National Congress, a South African political party and the main opponents of apartheid

Apartheid – The South African government's official title for its national segregation policy, beginning in the 1950s and ending in 1980

Afrikaner – White, usually Dutch, member of the South African ruling class before and during apartheid

Askari - A policeman, soldier, or trusted scout. In the case of elephants and Cape buffalos it is a younger bull sent from the herd with the older bull for its security.

Back (of the bow) – The side of the bow facing away from the archer when held normally

Bakkie – Afrikaans for pick-up truck

Biltong – Spiced strips of meat, cured by drying in air

Bosses – The broad heavy shield made by the base of the Cape buffalo horns at the top of its head

Belly (of the bow) – The side of the bow facing the archer when held normally

Boers – Descendants of Dutch settlers in South Africa.

Boma – An outdoor gathering and dining area, usually a fire pit with chairs and a dining area covered by thatch or canvas

Broadhead – An arrowhead with sharpened sides intended to kill by penetration and hemorrhage

Buff – Slang for Cape buffalo

Bwana – A master or top boss, also slang for great hunter

Curls – The lower portion of a Cape buffalo's horns that curl and end in a tapered point.

Dagga Boy – An old bull that has been kicked out of the herd. The word Daga means mud. These old bulls can typically be found in and near mud wallows.

Double rifle, or Double – A rifle with two barrels, typically mounted side by side but sometimes one over the other.

Fletching – Feathers at the rear of an arrow to stabilize its flight.

Glassing – Using binoculars to scan landscape

GoGo – A grandmother

Hide – Hunting blind, constructed so it covers the hunter's shape and movement.

Kudu – An African antelope that has a grayish or brownish coat with white vertical stripes. The male has long spirally curved horns.

Loose – To release the string of a bow or release an arrow from the bow.

Pap - Cornbread

Rand – South African currency

Riser – The center or body of a bow consisting of the handle, arrow shelf, that fades or tapers into the upper and lower limb

Wind/winding/winded – An animal detecting or alerting to the scent of human or other foreign odor